exurbia
Durham Academy Literary & Arts Magazine

2023-2024

editors

Madeline Gottfried '24

Katelyn Miller '24

Taylor Winstead '24

Ethan Li '25

faculty adviser

Dr. Lauren Garrett

I believe there's nothing more human, nothing more beautiful, than contemplating our existence; seeing the harsh truth and injustice of the world, and continuing to contemplate and create anyways. To be human is to explore all the aspects of the past and present, and to find something new and amazing in the cruel mundanity of reality. I am honored to bear witness to this and more through my time reading your poems, seeing your art, and being able to turn it into Exurbia. Never stop finding and creating beauty; this simple act of rebellion I encounter in the power of creativity is what keeps us human; it is what saves the world piece by peace. When you find yourself drowning in hate, remember that there is always something beautiful tucked away in a hidden corner of the world, in your mind. You just have to set it free.

♡ Madeline Gottfried '24

I'm so grateful for the opportunity to be able to work on such a cool project! It has been so amazing to see everyone's wonderful work and to be able to incorporate so much beauty into the journal. It's been quite the journey and I'm so excited to show you all what we've been working on all year. Thank you to Dr. Garrett, our amazing advisor, without whom we would've never been able to do this project. Thank you to the three other editors, Taylor, Madeline, and Ethan, and all the incredible work they have accomplished over the past year. Finally, thank you to all the amazing artists, photographers, and writers who gave us the opportunity to use their work. Art truly is something that brings us all together, which is something the OA community desperately needs. I hope this journal can be a step towards building a stronger and more supportive community.

with love,
Katelyn Miller

The arts have gotten me through the hardest moments of my life. Singing has given me a voice in dark times, performing has provided me with community... and art and writing have given me spaces to process my thoughts and feelings. The journal this year is filled with some incredible pieces. I am blown away by the talent of DA, and by the creativity, vulnerability, pain, and joy that the community has allowed us to present in this year's journal.

    I have had so much fun, and learned so much working with this year's editors. Thanks so much to Katelyn, Madeline, and Ethan for being such a fantastic team, and for all the wonderful work you contributed to the journal. Finally, huge thanks to Dr. Garrett - you have been so supportive throughout my time at DA, and I have been grateful for this chance to work with you!

    I hope you enjoy the journal, and thanks to all of you who submitted!

    Sincerely,
      Taylor

I would've been surprised if you had told my soph. self that I was an Exurbia editor this year — I used to avoid the ambiguity of art and prose in favor of anything with an answer key. As I flip through this year's edition, though, I know better.

Reading Exurbia offers brief windows into people we walk by every day between classes but who we don't really know much about. Through their submissions, you'll get to see very personal glimpses into individual experiences that combine to form the collective attitude of a DA student body that often prefers to keep it to themselves. Us editors choose how to put together that collective picture, and I'm so proud of how we've done it this year. Madeleine, Katelyn, & Taylor — thank you for showing me the ropes and welcoming me as the lone junior (and guy). Dr. G — thank you for being the glue that keeps us together, and your encouragement meant the world. I'm so excited to do this all again next year...

— Ethan Z.

table of contents

cover art

Rachel Pellom '24

prose

27   the careful art of dreaming up a better world — Madeline Gottfried '24

44   mountain story — Lily Carlson '24

75   the ocean must remain still — Katelyn Miller '24

82   medium — John McGowan '24

88   the death of math — Dr. Andrew Prudhom, faculty

108   screw you, old man — Jordan Adair, faculty

114   injuries of time — Madeline Gottfried '24

118   monetizing happiness — Taylor Winstead '24

126   arodnap mansion — Taylor Winstead '24

129   how i pass the time in despair — Lily Zellman '24

poetry

2   the graveyard tango — Blake Roper '24

7   ode to girlhood — Madeline Gottfried '24

17   wedding — Blake Roper '24

21   prism girl — Kiersten Hackman '24

24   lord of the fly — Kiersten Hackman '24

34   déliquescence — Priya Aggarwal '25 & Kathryne Hong '25

39   even a shrimp will change — Madeline Gottfried '24

42   her — Kiersten Hackman '24

59   greed and guts — Anonymous

63   guests who (couldn't) stay — Kiersten Hackman '24

66   the nut and the tree — Hannah Elman '27

70   the death of me — Anonymous

72   the long walk home — Katelyn Miller '24

81   hell in a handbasket — Taylor Winstead '24

85   i ate augustus — Blake Roper '24

86	canción primavera — Tony Valera '26	47	Whitney Wiles '25	105	Catherine Gao '24
87	fire escape — Azif	60	Catherine Gao '24	106	Mirabelle Smaini '26
96	i am a tree — Chloe Bidgood '25	62	Katelyn Miller '24	107	Milo King '24
101	scarab — Katelyn Miller '24	64	Catherine Gao '24	113	Catherine Gao '24
104	so now — Taylor Winstead '24	65	Olivia Rivers '24	115	Catherine Gao '24
110	her song — Taylor Winstead '24	68	Catherine Gao '24	117	Sol Dhungana '25
112	melt together — Blake Roper '24	74	Catherine Gao '24	119	Taylor Winstead /24
116	woman of fewer words — Blake Roper '24	75	Kilian Sadowski de Prada '25	123	Sol Dhungana '25
122	the lost canto — Ananya Mettu '26, Audrey Crowder '26, Fiona Lawton '26, Joanna Yoon '26	85	Anderson Levin '26	128	Catherine Gao '24
		89	Sophie Williamson '27	131	Margaret Jester '24
147	(I'm sorry) — Kiersten Hackman '24	90	Olivia Rivers '24	134	Olivia Rivers '24
		92	Margaret Jester '24	146	Taylor Winstead '24
		94	Margaret Jester '24	148	Margaret Jester '24
		95	Margaret Jester '24	149	Margaret Jester '24

visual art

1	Vincent Cao '26
3	Olivia Rivers '24
6	Madeline Gottfried '22
11	Erin Lee '24
22	Olivia Rivers '24
97	Ashley Slomianyj '26
98	Olivia Rivers '24
99	Ashley Slomianyj '26
102	Sol Dhungana '25
103	Sol Dhungana '25

photography

4	Rachel Pellom '24	58	Amelia Fay '25	121	Rachel Pellom '24
14	Rachel Pellom '24	61	Rachel Pellom '24	124	Rachel Pellom '24
16	Rachel Pellom '24	67	Amelia Fay '25	127	Evan Fields '24
18	Rachel Pellom '24	69	Milo King '24	133	Rachel Pellom '24
20	Mai Malesky '25	71	Rachel Pellom '24	141	Evan Fields '24
25	Rachel Pellom '24	73	Rachel Pellom '24	150	Grayson Auman '25
26	Milo King '24	79	Mai Malesky '25	151	Grayson Auman '25
31	Rachel Pellom '24	80	Amelia Fay '25		
33	Rachel Pellom '24	83	Rachel Pellom '24		
35	Milo King '24	84	Rachel Pellom '24		
37	Rachel Pellom '24	86	Rachel Pellom '24		
38	Rachel Pellom '24	89	Rachel Pellom '24		
41	Rachel Pellom '24	90	Amelia Fay '25		
43	Rachel Pellom '24	91	Amelia Fay '25		
50	Rachel Pellom '24	93	Amelia Fay '25		
54	Rachel Pellom '24	100	Amelia Fay '25		
55	Amelia Fay '25	111	Mai Malesky '25		

dedicated to Mr. Jordan Adair,
master teacher, lifelong learner,
writer, storyteller, lifesaver,
friend

Vincent Cao '26

the graveyard tango
Blake Roper '24

We have no stage, we have no cake
But a disco ball, the moon will make
For music, we all sing and cheer
We'll each sing a song from our own year.

The ruckus of ratt'ling holds the beat
It rattles down the silent street
These old bones will jive and dance
Over the stones we leap and prance.

All the boys, Kim does impress
With her torn, but pretty party dress
But all of us do flaunt and flirt,
For any old rag can be a good skirt.

We all find partners, mine was Lou
In his sailors suit, all torn and blue
We all jive while our joints all jangle
The tango makes our bones all tangle

Little Suzie jives alone
But soon finds new friends made of bone
No one weeps or feels any sorrow,
The last night of our lives will begin again tomorrow!

We all dance and we all sing
From dusk 'till dawn though summer and spring
Through winter and fall, we rattle with kin
For it gets quite cold without our skin.

Olivia Rivers '24

Rachel Pellom '24

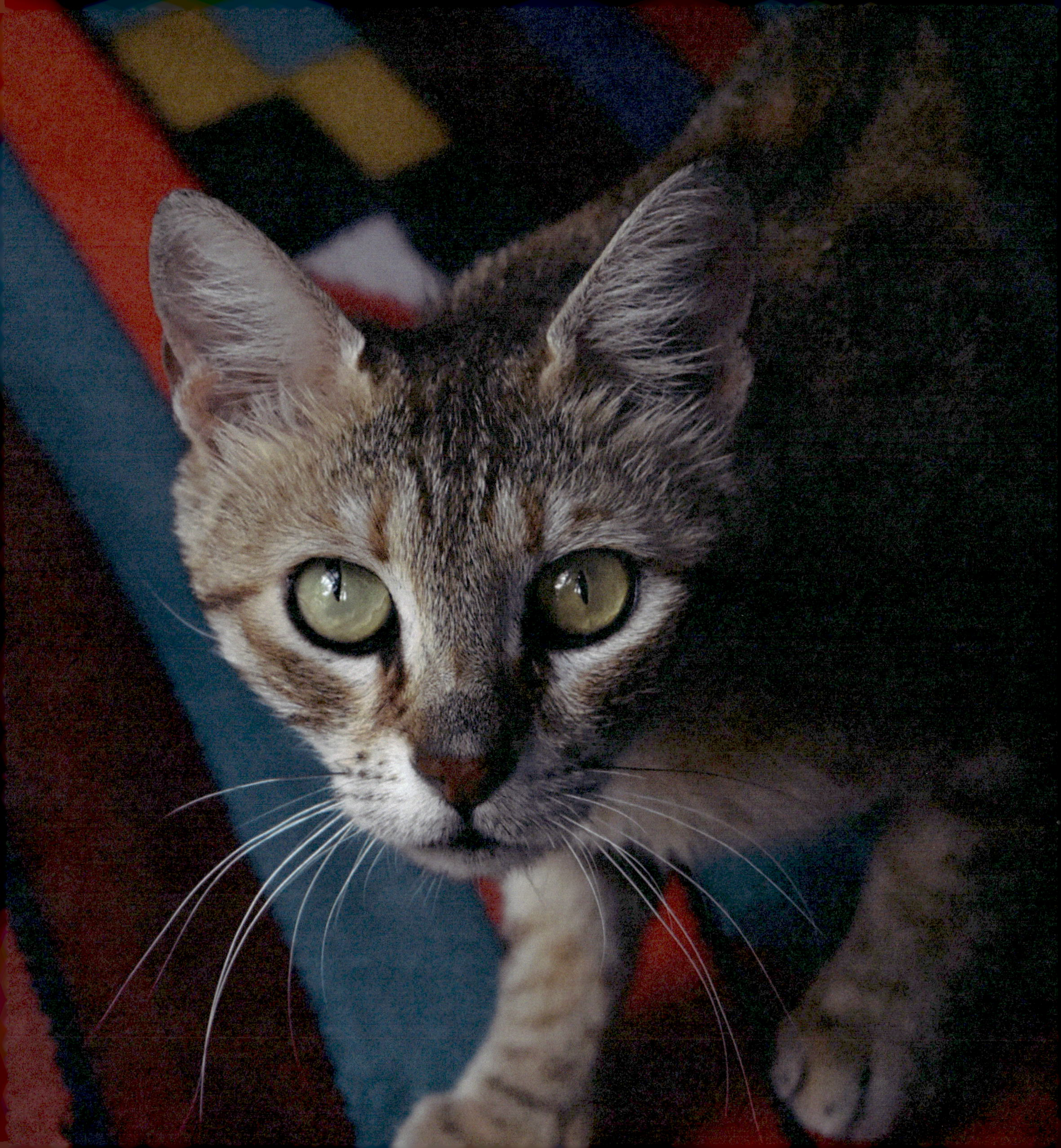

Madeline Gottfried '24

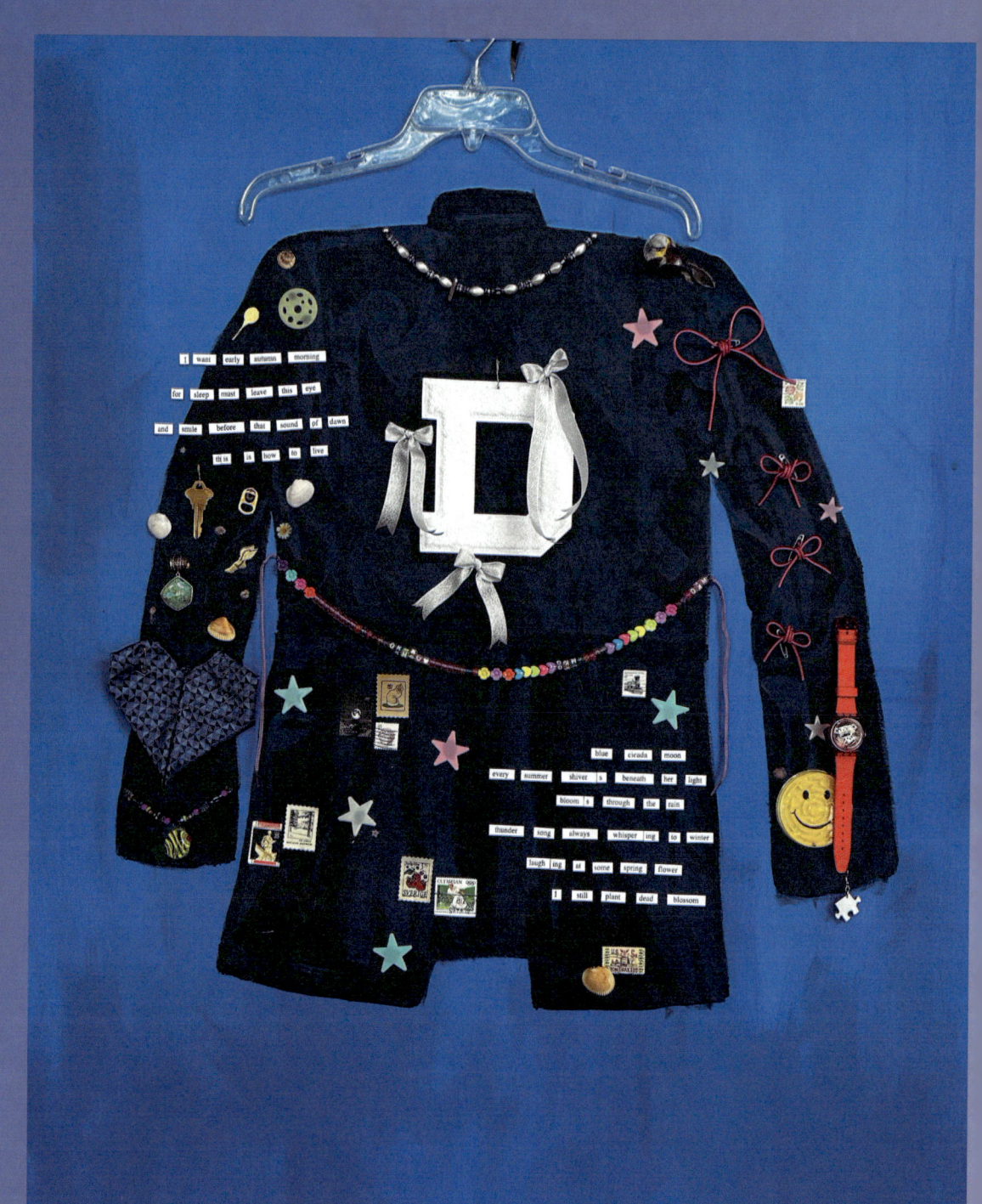

ode to girlhood
Madeline Gottfried '24

      1.   for me

I'm just a girl!
I glower at the stares of strange men on the street
and the only thought of impending doom
is that of future lines,
creasing my face into an everlasting look of death.

I'm just a girl!
the cuts in my legs are sewn up with ribbons rather than medical thread
Where's the fun in science, anyways?
no poetry in something as mundane as HIPPA violation or a hippocampus.

I'm just a girl!
I thank the modern era for runway shows and romanticization of pomegranates.
for the ability to say, "I read an article about this and that"
only to begin quoting a tiktok I saw the day before.

I'm just a girl!
my longest lasting memories of middle school are some of the following:

It's seventh grade and my friend grabs my hand while I walk to tell a boy I like him
and all I can think about is how to stall the visit
so her hand remains in mine.

It's sixth grade and it's ten minutes before we need to leave the house for school and I'm sitting on the beige carpet floor
sobbing and breathing faster than I knew I could because the drawers in front of me hold nothing but clothes that enrage me and I don't have a clue what to do.

It's fifth grade and I'm walking five feet off the ground along the fence before I slip
and fall onto the leaves
still wet from yesterday's snow.
and look down to see my left arm crooked in two new directions.

It's eighth grade and I've just exited the bathroom right by my advisory
in which I was plagued by the battle of which bra to wear for ultimate frisbee practice
and I connect my headphones to listen to my current favorite Twenty One Pilots song before I walk down to the field.

It's seventh grade and I'm sitting at a table by the pool, trying to keep my dripping, chlorinated hair
From contaminating the birthday card displaying heartfelt art
And a message of "I hope I get to see you more next year!"
from the girl who I ran around with every day during recess.
I guess we had different definitions of friendship.

I'm just a girl!
I hold nothing but hate in my heart for my past self that yelled back at my mother.
to put it in words I understand–
A concept she would undoubtedly lecture me for– she's just a girl.
she's a mother, maybe not the best one, or even a girl that should have been a mother.
but I have a hard time believing that it's her fault.
forgiveness is in this year, anyways.

I'm just a girl!
I have to come to terms with this middle school self, who I hated for so long.
I have to recognize that being 13 isn't a crime, certainly isn't a privilege, but is a stepping stone to becoming who I'm meant to be.
whoever she is.

And yet, I sit alone in bed and
cry and
cry.
my mother curses my name
calls me manic
says I can be happy, content.
All I have to do is try.

She doesn't get that I'm just a girl!
I'm trying my best
but I'm stuck in the middle of the sea
(what is girlhood other than an obsession with the ocean?)
isolated on a boat

and I'm just a girl! so maybe the ocean is filled entirely by my tears
maybe if it weren't for you and you
and you and
it would be just a puddle.

and I love the modern era because my pain, my sadness,
Well, it's chic. It's in.
eye bags are cute.
clean girl has been replaced by indie sleaze
by a revival of heroines doused in heroin chic.
and so I dress my wounds in these trends.
and the shards of my existence are haphazardly synthesized into scribbles in the notes app.

the season will change. I'll leave the beach hoping that joy will return while those horrid jean shorts and panic attacks that left me curled up on the hardwood floor
stay behind.

but I'm just a girl
So all I can do is hope

    2.   for her

I'm just a girl!
As soon as I could drive, my dream was to take my sister out for a ride after dinner, and to just coexist with the windows down and enjoy my music together.

When this dream finally came true, she was silent the whole time.
in a stale silence.
a worried silence.
and so I asked what was wrong and she told me she thought mom would get mad for us taking so long to return.
not exactly the happy ending I'd hoped for.
(she hated my music, too)

I'm just a girl!
We talk about how she looks at the errors me and my brother made, and how they shape her to be better than the both of us.

What can I say? If I were my parents, she'd be my favorite too.
but
she's too independent.
she's too stubborn.
she's too emotional.

Despite her efforts, she's too much like me.

and I love her too much.
when the house is filled with warring mothers and brothers and silent fathers,
She's in my room.
As I desperately cling onto any bit of happiness I can pass along to her.

I'm just a girl!
I'm her sister, mother,
I'm her friend, I'm her mentor, I'm her guardian, I'm her personal stylist.
I'm her sister.
and I'm not perfect.
I tell her what I think and
she cries.
and I'm so used to her being driven to tears that I'm numb to it.
(It's too similar to the tears I cried countless times in my youth)
(I was always too sensitive)
My mom scolds me:
"what will you do when I'm dead? will you two finally be close?"
because my sister only talks to her about me when I'm
not perfect.

So it's hard to know if she loves me
when it really matters.
When the stars fall off her ceiling walls
and the posters have long since been removed from mine.
And she whispers to a friend or lover
countless memories of me and her together
when the fights would never end
and I had to tell her, "Mom will come back. She just needs space.
I promise."

Erin Lee '24

Or will I just be the enemy that my mom so desperately wants her to see me as.

My mom and her sister didn't grow up close. but they were just girls.
and now me and my sister have to see what they've done
and change. Evolve. Just
try. because we're just girls!
so we must perform in this generational game,
seeking– blindly–
to find the balance between a multitude of roles in our little royal court.
and juggle them all.
perfectly.

I'm just a girl!
I know what i did wrong,
I know what my mom did wrong.
Yet here we remain.
with nothing but love as an excuse

       3.   for him

I'm just a girl! you hurt me time and time again
and all I can think is how
It's my fault!
I ask for too much!
you can't change, so I'll do it!
my mom says I need to change, so that I don't carry it with me for the rest of my life.
I can't have a face of "I need direct communication and for you to understand when I'm upset without having to explain it to you" for the rest of my life, right?

I know that you can hurt me time and time again,
but all I'll remember is how you held me close to your side while we brushed our teeth.

I know I'll remember how we stood on the bleachers watching a horrible soccer game
then he slapped you across the face
and your nose began to bleed
so I slapped him back and stormed away
holding your hand.

I know I'll never forget when you jokingly slapped me a little too hard and i had to stare at you with
tears in my eyes and ask you to never do that again.

I know you'll forget. I'm the one who never forgets. You can't seem to hold onto anything permanent from your past.
I'm just a girl! so I know exactly why you're the way you are.
and I know I can't stand your distance from intellectual connection.
I'll ponder the stars while you search for airplanes.
Poor boy, nobody ever told you where the stamp of affection seals onto the envelope!
but nobody told me either.
And I still know what to say when you get an email from him,
the man you haven't talked to in years.

I'm just a girl! so despite my romanticization of the mundane,
I fail to make sense of your occasional bouts of poetry–
"if there's no sense there's no sense, but I still love you"
"our own paradise in moonlight"
– you turn me into an illiterate writer
plagued by my own existence outside of yours.
Even if your entire existence, the compass guiding your life, will never point the same direction as mine.

I'm just a girl! you're my world,
and I have no way of knowing if I'm yours.
I won't sleep in the hoodie you dishearteningly removed from your closet, I'll just hold it so tight
that when I wake up, my arms will be sore.
Am I that wrong for wanting to hang on to the only tangible representation
of this painful love you've gifted me?

4.   and for them

I'm just a girl! as a tribute to all those before me who lived in a time
 where it was best to be anything but
just a girl.

george, ellis,
acton, and more.
I wish you didn't have to hide behind the name of another.

4.   and for them

I'm just a girl! as a tribute to all those before me who lived in a time
 where it was best to be anything but
just a girl.

george, ellis,
acton, and more.
I wish you didn't have to hide behind the name of another.

overt yet opaque,
their words fall on deaf ears, as the woman who needs to hear them most
just sees the writing of yet
another tiresome, contradictory man.
not adding, not subtracting. reduced to net neutral.
the system not displaced, history merely erased.

For them, I'm just a girl.
I still have to fight against a double mind, double bind.
Not your girl, but my girl.
viewed by an external, a window, a mirror.
As they see what I share, in the posters on my wall
or the mini skirt I desperately hold down as I walk up the stairs.
they see me, but I merely reflect what the outside already believes:
just,
a girl.

Rachel Pellom '24

Rachel Pellom '24

wedding
Blake Roper '24

Less complicated
When we dated, kindergarten
Picking flowers from the garden
For our wedding

18

Rachel Pellom '24

Mai Malesky '25

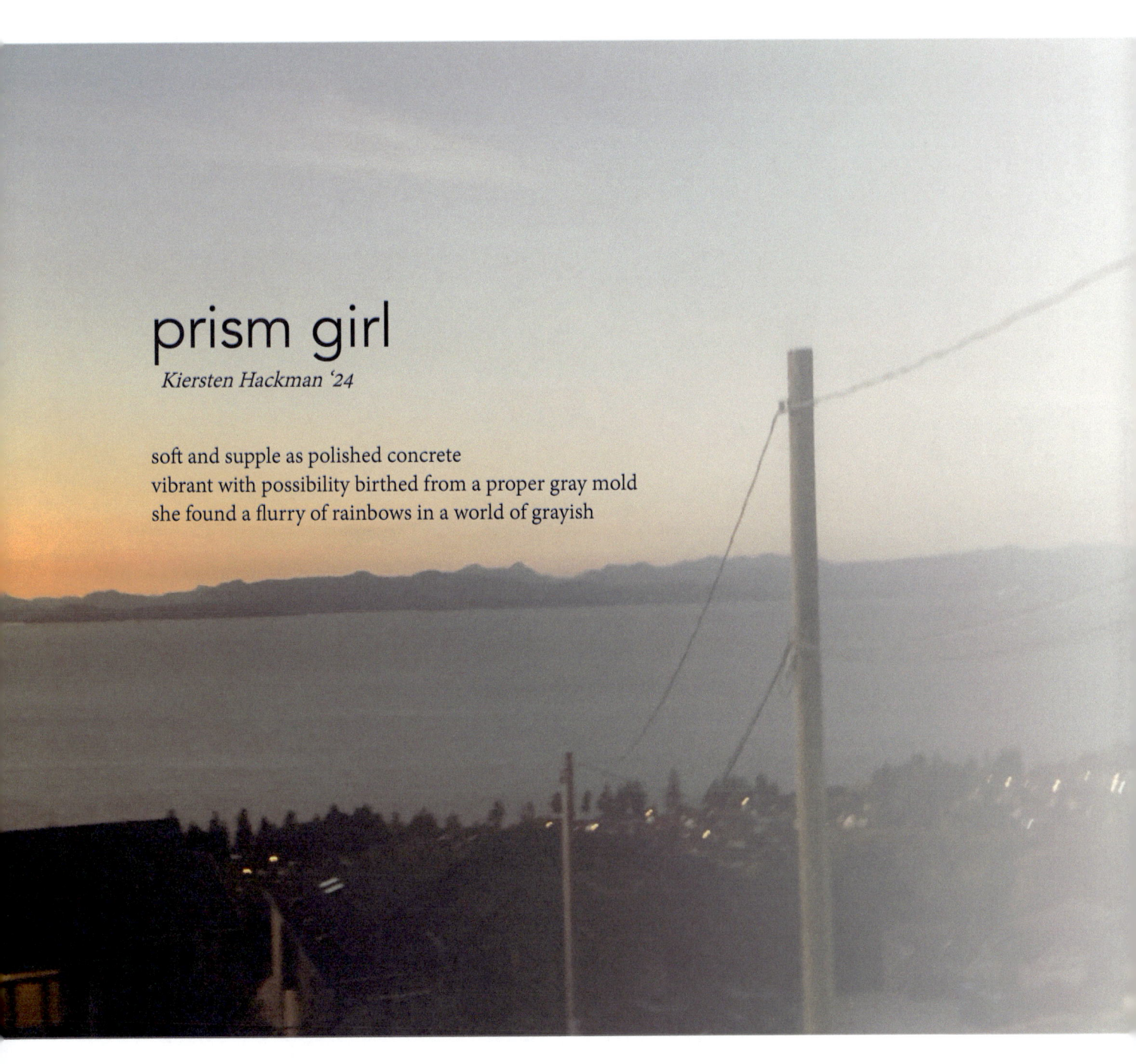

prism girl
Kiersten Hackman '24

soft and supple as polished concrete
vibrant with possibility birthed from a proper gray mold
she found a flurry of rainbows in a world of grayish

Olivia Rivers '24

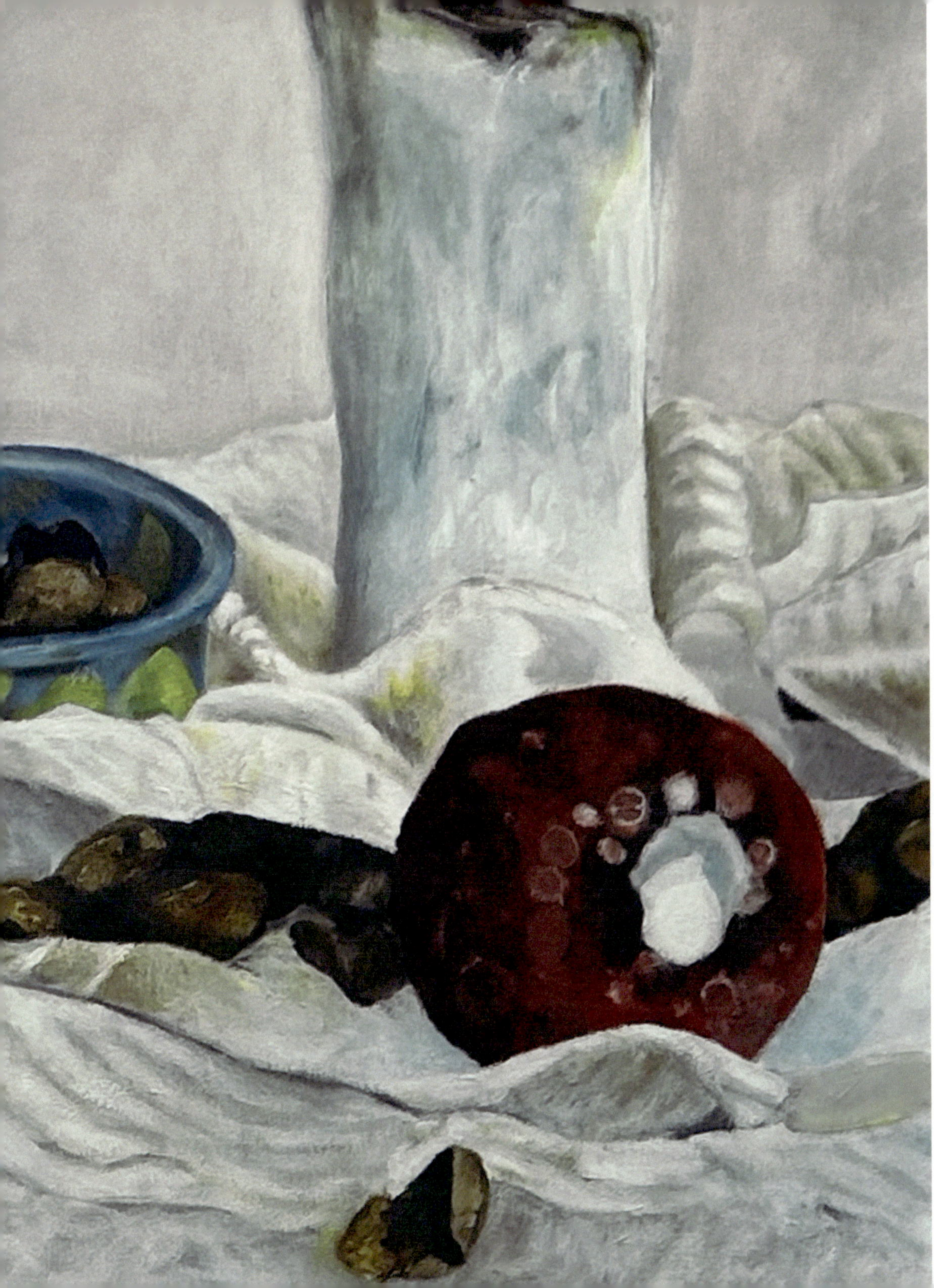

lord of the fly

Kiersten Hackman '24

she said
i have places to be
and thought he wouldn't touch her but to him she was
a bug in a bell jar
because his science textbooks said
she didn't have a place to be
outside his magnifying gaze. because he had constructed
glass walls around her in his mind, and when he looked through her
he saw only the reflection of himself, distorted into a god.
to him,
she was birthed the moment she
came into his presence,
and dust in the wind once he left.
so he pressed down on her
glass ceiling
and crushed her beneath his own
two palms.
and when he peeled off her wings
to press between the pages of his collection
and lay out —careful
in the spot he'd saved by the Spider's silk,
her body was discarded to the dry summer wind.

Rachel Pellom '24

Milo King '24

the careful art of dreaming up a better world

Madeline Gottfried '24

"Jane! Jane! You're finally home. Can we talk about my project? I have another idea."

Jane had only stepped in and shut the front door before Addison had appeared around the corner.

"Sounds good," Jane said with a smile. "Tell me everything."

"Let's go to the office first," Addy said, grabbing her sister's hand and guiding her towards the work table pressed against the wide, front window of the living room.

This table had a running joke between Addison and Jane's parents as being their third child; over the years, it had mysteriously morphed into a being of its own. It had been picked up at a garage sale, and purchased through the hormonal and delirious state of being that Charlotte, their mother, had floated in during her time pregnant with Jane. This impulsive purchase appeared to lack a purpose, as they had been gifted a lovely dining table nearly a year before by a mutual friend who hand crafted it when faced with uninspiring options in the wedding registry. Nonetheless its presence– always covered in some assortment of books, from basic phonetics to unquestioningly great classics– remained undisputed in the back of holiday and prom photographs alike.

Jane's second-grade creativity and brief stint into geometric abstraction, before her deep appreciation for impressionism had begun, had covered the top left corner with stickers shaped in yellow stars, blue squares, red triangles, and orange hexagons. Jane had a nervous habit of picking and peeling at the shapes, which Addy would always scold her for as she sought to preserve those marks of a seemingly simpler time for sisterly bonds.

Addy sat down in her beloved blue chair, and Jane took a moment to revel in the state of perfection it managed to exist in. Addy had never been a reckless toddler, as she always adored and mirrored the style– from dress to vocabulary– of Jane; thus, skipping over the era of destroying LEGO buildings and pulling grass out of the lawn that her classmates had experienced. Jane sat down across from Addy, and her younger sister began to present her project's thesis.

"I can picture it perfectly," Addy stated, emphatically pressing the palms of her hands on the table. "When I'm older, we'll live in a house together, wherever we want to. We'll be just like us now, only grown up. We will read outside on the front porch and talk about the interesting things we learn over tea and snacks. We won't take up all our time complaining about our jobs like Mom and Dad do, because we'll just do what makes us happy!"

Jane paused, checking that Addy had finished, before sighing, subtly shaking her head, and replying.

"Addy, I don't think that works. You can't write a paper about a future like that! I worry that all it would do would make your teacher and class laugh at you. I'm sure all your friends are writing about the job you want or what you'll have done in high school. Why don't you give that a try?"

Addy crinkled her brows at her sister's response.

"But that's the other kids. The assignment is to write about where I see myself in the future."

Jane tried to remain calm. She had to recognize that this was not a battle of who was right and who was wrong, but rather Jane's desperate attempt to protect her beloved sister from the outside world. She'd seen classmates sporting unpopular, but not controversial, perspectives thrive, simply by hiding a small bit of themselves. She had traded in aspects of her artistic side for a life of tranquility, and all she wanted was for her sister to be able to do the same.

And yet alongside this, she realized that she was the one making her sister feel silly and stupid just for having a different vision of the future. Jane sighed, and tried to start over.

"Your world sounds amazing. I would love to grow old with you by my side. But that's just not how it works. There's no way to afford a house all on our own, and even if they say otherwise, I know mom and dad want us to have families of our own one day."

Addy paused, and looked at her sister, eyes wide with an abundance of emotions on the brink of overflowing.

"Jane, why are you so worried about what others will think?"

"Because it's selfish to not think about how we need to add to the world around us! Our actions have power, so we must understand that a choice to separate ourselves from the outside world might give us joy, but will still harm others in the end."

"No. No. Think, please," Addy said, yet again speaking much slower than the rush of words that dumped out of Jane's mouth moments before. Jane forced herself to relax back in her seat before she looked up at her sister, and began to truly heed her words.

"I don't want to spend my whole life thinking about what's going through everyone else's mind. That sounds exhausting. But it doesn't have to be as extreme as you make it out to be; it doesn't have to be my dream against everyone else's hopes for me. You know how much I want to make the world a better place for me, for us, but that doesn't have to come at the cost of everything falling apart."

It seemed that now it was Jane's turn to stare at her sister, paralyzed by the complexity her sister had brought to this seemingly simple situation. How had a school assignment sparked such a discussion? That's Addy's power; she knows how to see through things to the deeper, and often the deepest, levels. And she should never have to hide it. Because it was, quite frankly, what made her better than the rest.

Maybe it didn't matter how she would be seen. Jane's first instinct had been to justify her own vision, rather than honor the new, and honestly better, idea that Addy presented. And all she'd done was blame everyone else. In the end, it was her, not their parents, not a teacher, not a classmate, that was telling Addy this. There was no one else to blame but herself.

And what was she doing? Going on about how her intentions were pure, when what she was really doing was killing a dream, a dreamer, the biggest dreamer of them all. Jane knew she was stubborn, just like her mother and father, but Addy was motivated. She couldn't be blinded by an idea of being right and her sister being wrong; all she wanted was to stay intent on her goals, on her vision.

Jane snapped back to reality and pushed back the corner of the star sticker she had subconsciously been peeling up. She looked up into the clarity and determination outwardly expressed on her sister's face, and knew that all she had to say for Addy to understand was, "I love you."

And so she did.

"I love you too, Jane," Addy said, a smile leaping up to the sides of her mouth.

Addy picked up a pink pencil, and began to write. Jane had no way to know what exactly she would say or what would happen in class when she shared her ideas out, assuming she hadn't done so already. But what did that matter? Addy was happy, and she was happy. It was just a paper anyways.

Acton and Charlotte stood still in the kitchen backs pressed against the lower island as they silently listened to their daughters finish their discussion and begin their homework.

"How'd it get to be like this?" Acton asked, turning around with his head down and pressing his hands against the cool marble countertop.

"What do you mean?" Charlotte responded, mirroring his movement.

Acton pulled his hands up and spun his ring around his finger. She watched his careful movements as he thought through his next words.

"They used to be so close. Don't you remember how Addy used to look up to Jane? The games they would play together."

He brought his hand up to his brow in distress, opening and closing his mouth before starting again.

"I still remember the world they built with the coup in the fairy kingdom. Jane had just learned about the French Revolution, and Addy had stumbled across an old encyclopedia of mythical creatures, leading to an unexpected combination. They would race around the backyard, doused entirely in glitter, screaming at the top of their lungs about how the royal family must pay for what they'd done. I miss how they didn't know how much they were terrifying us, or the poor neighbors for that matter. They haven't smiled the same since then. I fear they've lost the connection they had back then."

Charlotte looked into his eyes and let her mind wander alongside his words. She knew he was wrong, but she knew she had to walk down memory lane with him to truly understand.

"I don't think they've changed as much as you think they have. They still love each other just as much, they've just grown up. Do you remember the battle over naming the fish? The endless weeks filled with lists with pros and cons to each one? Just for a bird to sneak into the kitchen and steal it away. Oh, they laughed so hard whenever we reminded them. Or when we ran out of photos to place into the frames, so there was a stock image alongside those of our family? Emily, they named her. I can't remember if we got so tired with their incessant stories that we finally removed the photo."

She paused, caught up in a whirlwind of memories of the youth of her children. She recognized the superficial change Acton might see in their daughters, especially Jane, who despised the hikes and jelly shoes that her upbringing was riddled with. No, now she was a troubled artist, stifled by the group of friends she had deliberately chosen. Everything had to be certain and serious with her, each part of her life a puzzle piece put into place to align perfectly with those around it. Her clothes must match, her hair must fall in the perfect wave, she must correct every mistake on her biology test, and Addy had to follow this path of perfection.

Charlotte saw this part most in her eldest daughter; yes, she put excessive amounts of pressure on herself, but all so Addy could continue to look up to her. This part of girlhood, unlike Jane's safety blanket which had traveled the lengths of the world, only to reach an eventual demise in the hallway closet, would never be left behind. And that was something Acton would never be able to understand. Their daughters would always choose each other over the rest of the world.

With this final thought, she began, "It's not our job to judge their dreams or personalities, we just have to trust that we've set them up for success. In the end it's about them, not us," she said cooly, taking her time to fully communicate each word. "I will not be the one to decide that Addy's dream is any less important than another. All we can do is hope and try that she is able to accomplish it. Just because her vision is different doesn't mean it's any less important. We love them both more than they will ever know, and in the end, that is what matters." Acton looked back at Charlotte's unbreakable stare, and couldn't help but still feel worried for his children.

"Maybe," was all he could think to say.

He moved away from the counter and walked to lean against the kitchen's door frame. His wife followed suit, and he wrapped his arm around her waist, and they looked to where Addy and Jane sat at the work table. Jane alternated between furious glances towards her laptop, brightly displaying a periodic table, and rapidly scribbling in a worksheet tucked between the pages of her notebook. Her brows were crinkled, mirroring the face her mother frequently wore in moments of doubt or peril, and Charlotte couldn't help but smile at the similarity they were beginning to bear. Addy sat across from her sister, legs pulled into a tight cross on her chair, as she enthusiastically wrote sentence after sentence into her binder's loose leaf sheets of paper. Charlotte and Acton didn't have a clue what would happen to their daughters, but in that moment, as they looked at the determination openly displayed on the faces of the bright girls in front of them, sitting at a table representing an emblem of both their youth and their parents, they understood that they would grow and change. But to love, to be loved, is to change, to evolve. And their daughters were twin vines wrapping around the same tree; they might go their own way, but when it mattered most, they'd find each other. And that was enough.

At last, Charlotte replied, extending the second syllable of each word before abruptly halting, "Maybe. Maybe." ♛

Rachel Pellom '24

Rachel Pellom '24

33

déliquescence

Priya Aggarwal '25 and Kathryne Hong '25

On était très sérieux, quand on a dix-sept ans, Un jour gris, foin des drogues et tabac
Des cafés vide à une pandémie
- On va sous les tilleuls pour se cacher d'un morne monde
Les tilleuls sentent graisseux les soirs stressants de juin! L'air est parfois maladif, qu'on ferme la paupière,
Le vent chargé de silence - il n'y a pas al ville ici -
Ades parfums de al grasse et des parfums de métal pourri...

I
- Voilà qu'on aperçoit une interne guerre pour les enfants D'azur feu, encadré des larmes bleu
Piqué d'une gaz hilarant, qui se fond
Avec des souffles vide, petite et toute désorientée
Nuit de juin! Dix-sept ans! - On se laisse griser
La poison est du champagne et vous monte àal tête. On divague; on se réveille aux lèvres un baiser Qui accumule là, comme un vomi écœurant.

III
Le coeur des enfants qui rejettent les romans
- Lorsque, dans al clarté d'un route déserte,
Passe une demoiselle aux petits airs épouvantables,
Sous l'ombre des personnes qui pourrissent après al pandémie
Et comme elle vous trouve immensément naif, Tout en faisant trotter dans les Gucci bottines
Elle se tourne, triste parce qu'elle ne peut pas le se permettre Mais pour l'argent li meurent
Back page has more! "

IV
Vous êtes amoureux. Parce que tu est matérialiste
Vous êtes amoureux. - Mais vous ne voulez pas vous attacher Tous vos amis s'en vont, ils sont mauvais goût.
- Puis l'adorée, un soir, a daigné vous écrire !...
- Ce soir-là..., - vous rentrez aux cafés vide,
Vous demandez des des drogues et tabac
- On est sérieux, quand on a dix-sept ans
Et qu'on a des tilleuls pour se cacher d'un morne monde

Milo King '24

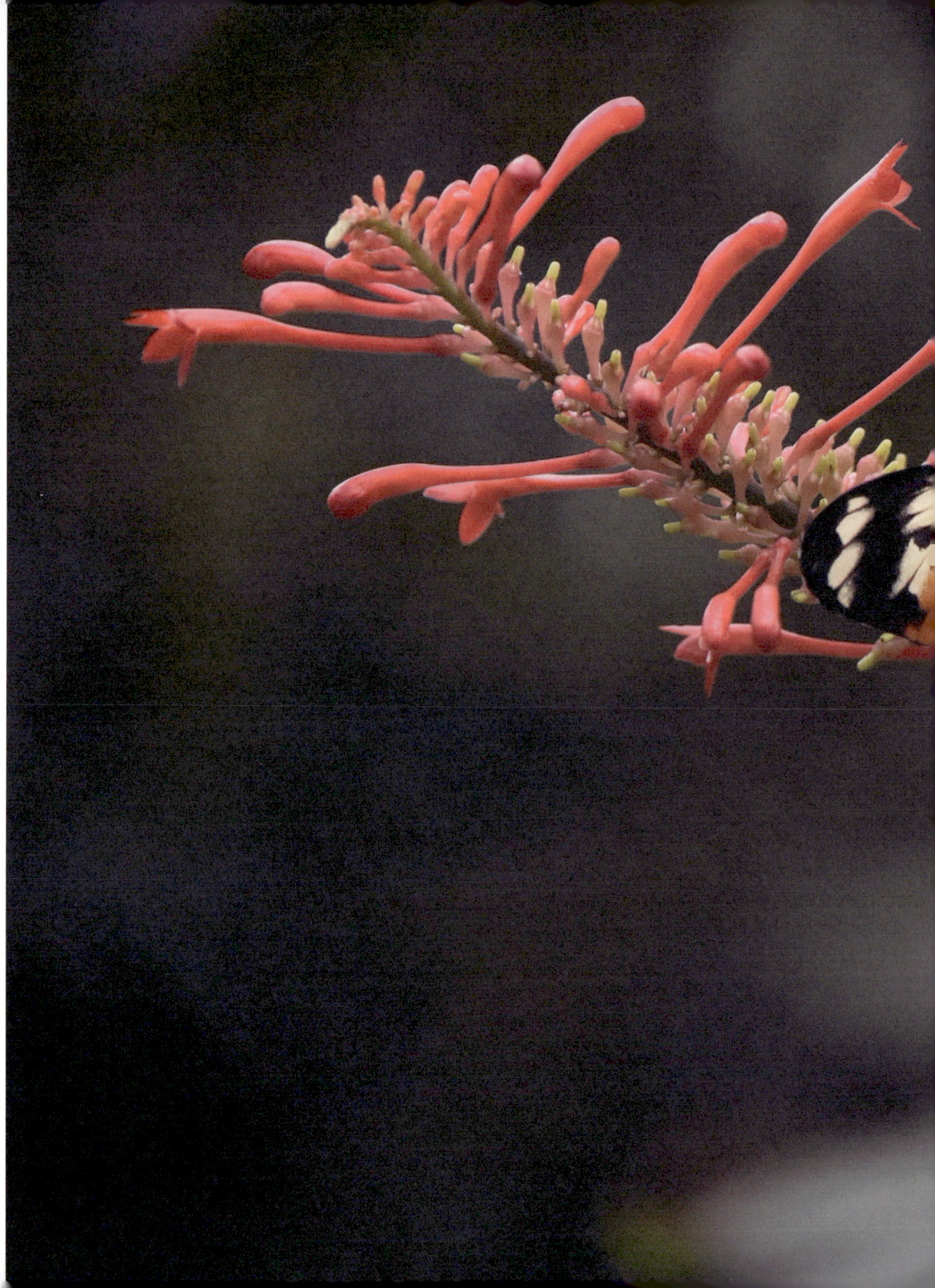

Rachel Pellom '24

Rachel Pellom '24

even a shrimp will change
Madeline Gottfried '24

and yet I find myself peeling back the layers of my existence.
agonizing over the joyful memories hidden behind complete and utter destruction.
The beauty I find is never what I set out looking for.
but what you least expect tends to end out hurting the most.
if I'm not tearing myself to pieces on the daily,
am I even close to reaching my potential?
I want to feel it all.

Nothing hurts quite as much as looking back at photos. The intimacy of a memory, even my own, like
licking honey off of knives
and praying for just one moment of sweetness.

I miss the time when we didn't know that we were supposed to know better,

but still
I love everything so deeply
and god it hurts
But I wouldn't change it for the world.

I can preserve my own livelihood surrounded by bright stars,
eyes flickering under fluorescent lights.
stray cats live.
you'll kill the bug
the true Icarus among us,
flying just too close to your ear.
and I'll cry in the backseat
mourning the loss of someone who didn't deserve to die.

but the birds still sing.

I'll make mistakes
I'll die trying
but I need to make, to try, to do.

I need to live.
And to live in every corner of the earth
there's wonder hidden in each crevice, you know,
and so I will see it.
I will listen to the song the universe sings to me.
I'll bookmark it,
add it to an album, then circle back to it at a time when I didn't know it would hurt the most.

In the end the sun is shining.
and I'm thinking of you.

If I could be anywhere
we'd be together.
Trapped in the summer of my memory.
but until I meet you again we'll hide in the meals we shared.
besides, I'll always hide you in my poetry.
I could never misplace your significance, no matter how cluttered my camera roll is.
So here, take this dried rose.
take this music box. she never played the song, but it was hers, and she's gone so it might as well be too.
one less thing for me to hide away.

I'm a dreamer
I'm a writer
I'll never let go of the broken pieces.
I'll crawl under my bed and look through the boxes,
my nostalgia will always be me.
I will never let go.
It will never be the last time, I'll lose myself again and again. but
it's nice to sit in the summer sun
to bask in the light.
it's warm. and just like that, oh, joy!
how I've waited for your return.

There are stars above my head and you're up there too.
there's a lot to think about when you remember everything ...

Rachel Pellom '24

... but whatever you do,
never take the advice of a poet.

her
Kiersten Hackman '24

like yolk spilling over the swollen crescent
of the horizon, she was a
showstopper.
the moon softened with her presence, the barest drop of
silver
lining her curls, alight with
night-magic swinging, singing like
coral bells, she walked like coral koi
swimming in her eyes, full and drinkable as sweet-tart
grenadine.

Rachel Pellom '24

mountain story
Lily Carlson '24

    The cupid on her right knee peaked out from under her dress every time she'd pedal further. Margot remembered the day she'd dipped that sewing needle into a messy pot of black ink and pressed it into that skin. She'd been so afraid to hurt her but Daphne had just pinched her skin and smiled as she tattooed. In the end it had turned out to be one of the best pieces she'd ever done. She liked that feeling of knowing its story, that small cupid on her friend's leg, as they biked to their spot.
    The late sun warmed the crowns of their heads as they cruised down the cobbled path to the river. It was dawn, the moon rising low over the horizon of mountain peaks. The sky was a warm summer indigo, as if it had been dyed by the Baptisia flowers that grew in every flower pot in their small town. A slow summer breeze met them at every turn in the road.
    Margot couldn't help but smile into the wind. It was her favorite time of the year, she was going to see her favorite people, and they were meeting at her favorite spot.
    "Keep your eyes on the road, silly. We won't make it if you crash," Daphne giggled back to her. Her eyes lit up in a way they never could during the school year. This was how youth was meant to be spent. Speeding through town on your bike in the dawn of a beautiful summer.
    When they finally reached the rusted gate to the river's small beach, Margot could make out the flashlights of the others in the sand already.
    "After you," she nodded to Daphne, looking at the gate.
    "Why thank you," Daphne grinned back. She gave herself a bit of space from the gate and then sprinted at it. One jump and she had made it up half the gate. After she maneuvered over the entire fence she waved Margot on. Margot repeated Daphne's actions, screaming a little when her foot almost slipped off a rung. When she hit the sandy ground of the beach, Daphne grabbed her hand and took off running towards the water, pulling her along.
    They didn't make it all the way to the shore though. Instead they were stopped by a circle of three kids, book bags piled in the center of their ring, the smell of cigarette smoke encasing them. Margot's heartbeat calmed from the running as she gazed upon the softly lit faces of her friends.
    "Do you ever run out of energy?" a dark haired girl, furthest from the two at the edge of the group, asked Daphne.
    "You know Astrid, I really don't think I do," Daphne retorted, flashing her the middle finger.
    "Aaaaand now that they're fighting, I know the group's finally all together," said a rusty voice, tinged with a Southern accent. The voice came from a shorter boy, hunched to the left of the circle of bags, pulling a cigarette out from between his lips.
    "I couldn't agree more Leo," Margot gave him a knowing look. She sat down between him and Daphne, every-

one readjusting to fit the two new bodies. Directly next to Daphne, a boy dressed in all black sat, arms wrapped around his knees, head tucked between his arms.

Margot leaned around Daphne and patted his arm.

"You okay, Max?" she asked softly. The boy's head popped up, his eyes glistened in the soft moonlight.

"Yeah yeah, I'm okay. Glad y'all are here." He gave a quiet, genuine smile. His hands fumbling in the sand next to him told a different story but Margot kept her mouth shut and turned to face forward again.

The white noise of the salty river blanketed the banter of the group. Daphne, as usual, was going on and on about some new love interest. Margot could only tell you that his name started with a B and he was exceptionally good at playing the trumpet. Leo seemed particularly adamant that she not get too invested.

"We're leavin' in a few weeks Daph, he's not stayin' here like you are," he warned.

"I know, it's not serious, I just…," her voice trailed off, eyes dropping from his. As she gazed endlessly into the now poorly lit sand of the beach, Margot could tell she meant it, it'd likely be over in less than a month. She also knew that this was Daphne's way of dealing with any problem she couldn't get rid of with spontaneous art projects or obsessions.

"C'mon Leo, leave her alone, let's just focus on us," Max called out, unfurling from his position.

"I agree, it's too pretty a night to get caught up in endings when we could be caught up in the present," Margot concurred. And they all agreed, telling stories from their week, laughing over old jokes and passing around chips and booze. It wasn't long until Margot's watch told her it was midnight. *Three hours had passed and it still wasn't enough time with them,* she thought to herself.

As Margot's hair frizzed from the warm salty air, the moon rose higher above the huddled circle of youth. Astrid had reached the point in her night when she pulled out her pack of Marlboros, carefully sifting through the cigarettes until she found the perfect one. If you asked her, she'd tell you she wasn't a smoker: her car never smelled it, her teeth were perfectly white, and no one but the group knew about this habit. Only on nights like this would the existential line of the sea hitting the sky provoke Astrid to light up, a habit Margot knew she had inherited from her dad.

Abruptly, Astrid, startled, dropped the selected cigarette from between her fingers as Daphne clicked on her flashlight, held it beneath her chin, and yelped at the group. She giggled as the group screamed, Leo scrambling to his feet and making it a good ways away before she called out to him.

"Leo, I just wanted to get you all scared, please come back, I have a story," she shouted, a maniacal grin seeping through her explanation.

"Yeah well you earned an A-fucking-plus, Daph," Leo exhaled, hands shaking, rejoining the group.

"All fun and games," Daphne giggled, the flashlight casting deep shadows across her face. "My story is what will really scare you … I'll begin then. I was minding my business, just a few days ago, walking around town, but someone caught my eye. A young woman, eyes lined in black, was talking in a doorway with someone who seemed to be her mother. Of course I listened …"

"Never minding her own business," Astrid rolled her eyes.

"Will you let me finish?" Daphne glared at her. "Her mom was talking about the biggest mountain."

"Like Mount Alice?" Margot asked.

"Yes," Daphne giddily replied, "Here's where it gets real. The mom told the girl that if she could make it to the top of Mount Alice in three nights, the mountain would allow her one wish that it would fulfill, no matter what."

"Sick," Leo said sitting up, "so, are there rules, or what?"

"I think I heard her say that you are not allowed to wish someone dead or alive. Nothing to do with that immortal bullshit. But like, realistic wishes, you know? I think I was meant to hear it. I think we have to go!" Daphne squealed.

"Absolutely not. I don't do hikes and that mountain is way too tall to climb that quickly," Astrid complained.

"I'm with Astrid. Honestly, with this group's work ethic we'd never make it," Max agreed.

"Hey, what the fuck, Max?" Daphne looked offended.

"I'm just saying, like Leo left the playing cards at home today because they were 'too much work to grab'. They were quite literally in his living room."

"Please don't expose me like that, Max. He's kind of right though, Daph. I don't know," Leo sounded skeptical, Astrid's arms were crossed in defiance, Max didn't look excited. Margot never loved hiking. It definitely wasn't her idea of fun, but the excitement that glittered in Daphne's eyes hit her in her heart. And to be completely honest, something in Margot had always believed the towering mountain at the edge of town held some sort of power, however fantastical.

"You guys, what the hell, it's our last summer together like this. If we can't handle a challenge like Mount Alice, are we gonna be able to handle college?" Margot said, standing.

That Friday the parking lot of the trailhead to Mount Alice's peak was filled with three cars and two bikes. The group had spent the week leading up to that Friday collecting supplies and gear. Luckily Daphne's dad used to be a frequent backpacker and had three used packs for the group to use along with two sleeping bags and two tents. Astrid and Leo volunteered to buy their own packs and sleeping bags and Margot already owned a sleeping bag from years of sleepovers when she was younger. Astrid put herself in charge of shopping for the food and gear after lengthy research on what's best to bring to save space.

Daphne wrote each of them a list of things to bring that her dad had put together for them: two t-shirts, two long sleeve shirts, one fleece jacket, one poncho, two pairs of shorts, two pairs of pants. When the lists were received, a lot of complaining about smelling bad was done, but Daphne told them all to get over it and they eventually complied.

At the trailhead Astrid emptied piles of cup noodles, instant oatmeal, bread, and peanut butter and jelly into one heap. In another heap she emptied a couple pots and backpacking stoves along with some utensils and gas tanks. Finally, in a third heap the tents and tarps were stacked.

"Alright, I want everyone to take an equal amount of gear. Remember, the way up is going to be — fingers crossed — a three-day hike. From there it's a one-day hike down the other side to a small rest area that has shuttles heading back to the trailhead. So, everyone needs to take four cup noodles, four packets of oatmeal, and then we'll split up the other food and gear equally by weight. Sound good?" Astrid explained to the group.

Everyone nodded their heads. "Yes ma'am!" called Leo. They all knew they wouldn't get anything done without Astrid. She was the only reason this trip was actually going to make it from plans to reality.

Whiteny Wiles '25

As they packed all of their gear into trash bags and then stuffed it into their packs, they giggled and reminisced. It was early morning but Daphne had brought them all coffees so the packing went by quickly. They were soon throwing their packs over their backs, Max falling over several times before finding a way to balance the weight. As it approached nine in the morning, the group began their journey.

The air was light and full of an excitement Margot felt running through her nerves. She couldn't stop smiling as they navigated the first sections of the trail. Astrid led, map in hand, having drawn out the route they needed to take with a sharpie. Max walked beside her and they conversed about some new book they both had read. Margot walked in the middle with Daphne, Leo taking up the rear.

"Do you remember the sophomore year camping trip?" Daphne asked the two.

"Oh my gosh, how could I forget. Becky H. and Henry holding hands while hiking? So crazy. And remember that massive spider in our tent?" Margot laughed remembering the absurdity of the school trip.

"Um, yes! It scared the living shit out of me," Daphne exclaimed.

"Wait, I remember your scream that the whole campsite heard. Like, I was on the other side of the site and I still heard you," Leo was laughing now too.

"I get the sense that this trip is going to be a little more difficult than the flat hiking, two-day camping trip of our past," Margot pointed out. They all nodded in agreement.

"To be honest, I'm a little nervous. I've never really done something like this before," Leo admitted, wringing his hands.

"You know, I was too. But I feel like if the motto of senior year isn't yolo, I don't know what it is. I feel so free to do anything right now, you know?" Margot comforted.

"I completely agree. Don't even worry, Leo, my dad made me take a list of solutions to most problems that would come up," Margot scoffed. "He's such a helicopter parent."

"Your dad? A helicopter parent? Have you met Mr. Hart?" Leo asked, almost offended at her suggestion.

"Shit, Leo, you're right. Your dad's leagues worse than mine, my bad," Daphne apologized. The group knew how hard Leo fought just to come on this trip. He had to promise his dad that the week after they came down, he wouldn't leave the house and would focus on scholarship essays. They all felt for him, but his father, Mr. Hart, commanded a fierceness none of them dared stand up to.

"Can we talk about something else?" Leo asked, embarrassed now.

"Of course Leo," Daphne patted him on the shoulder. "Do you guys know when we're stopping for lunch. I feel like it's definitely past noon."

"I'll go ask Astrid," Leo said, jogging up the slope they were on to the front.

"Do you think he's mad at me?" Daphne turned to Margot.

"No, Daph. You were making a joke and weren't thinking. He knows you hate his dad for the way he acts. I think acknowledging it is hard for him though."

"I know. He's gotta unpack all of that at some point though. I just hope he knows we're here for him when that time comes."

"He knows," Margot smiled reassuringly. Secretly, she was only saying that because she hoped it was true.

"Y'all check it out!" Leo called from the front, grabbing Astrid's arm and dragging her forward. Margot couldn't make out what he was so excited about until she turned a corner crowded with shrubs and all of the foliage cleared before her. She couldn't help but let out a small gasp at what she saw. In front of Leo was an expansive, glistening pool of water outlined by boulders that dwarfed the group. However, the most magical part Margot thought, was the cascading waterfall streaming out of the watering hole. It rushed violently over the rocky terrain of the cliffside ahead of them, falling into smaller and smaller pools of water until it reached some imminent end out of sight.

"Oh hell yes!" Daphne exclaimed, already tearing off her tank top and hiking shorts.

"Wait for me, Daph!" Margot called after her, dropping her pack to the ground stripping down to her sports bra but remaining in her running shorts. When the two girls reached the sandy edge of the pool they were giggling with exhilaration. Margot reached out a toe and dunked it in the water.

"Freezing!" She squealed.

"Nothing we can't handle," Daphne grinned, grabbing her hand. But before the two could leap into the cold water before them, they heard a loud, "woohooooo", and the glimpse of Leo's half-naked body flew past them, water splashing everywhere as he sprinted deeper into the pool.

"Leo," Margot rolled her eyes, held tighter to Daphne's hand, and the two joined him in the water, splashing about. They all paddled around together, floating on their backs and having splash fights. Leo lifted Daphne up on his shoulders, running her around until he waded too deep and they both sank into the water, Daphne yelling at him after they surfaced for almost drowning her.

But, Margot couldn't help but notice the way Leo's smile never faded from his face as he was looking at Daphne, even as she berated him. It was the same way he had looked at her since she'd met both of them at the beginning of freshman year. Eyes wide with some sort of astoundment, the edges of his mouth always turned up when she spoke, a slight pink surfacing on his tan cheeks whenever she touched him. Somehow all unnoticed by Daphne herself.

Margot shot Astrid a knowing look and Astrid just smirked back giving a breathy giggle. Both of the girls had caught on to Leo in their freshman year biology class. They weren't friends with Leo then, and almost every single one of his old friends were in the class with him. But so was Daphne. Every day his friends sat together in the back of the class at one table and Daphne, Astrid, and Margot sat together in the front at another. And every day Leo would wave to his friends and prance right over to the girls table, plopping himself right across from Daphne, next to Margot.

It was that same look that he gave her while she watched the lesson and he watched her, fingers playing nervously with his pencil, notebook in front of him empty. Astrid and Margot would give secret smiles across the table to each other every time she turned back to the group and Leo quickly dropped his gaze, scribbling nonsense notes, head down and cheeks flushed.

He never alluded to liking her vocally, keeping it to himself all these years as he watched her date other guys, dating other girls himself. His relationships never lasted more than a month or two though. Here he was, still in love, still too scared to say it. Margot could only hope their leaving would change that.

Astrid and Max sunbathed on one of the flatter boulders around the pool, snacking on pb&j's while Margot, Daphne, and Leo continued to swim around for hours. As the afternoon went on, Margot and Daphne got out and joined

Rachel Pellom '24

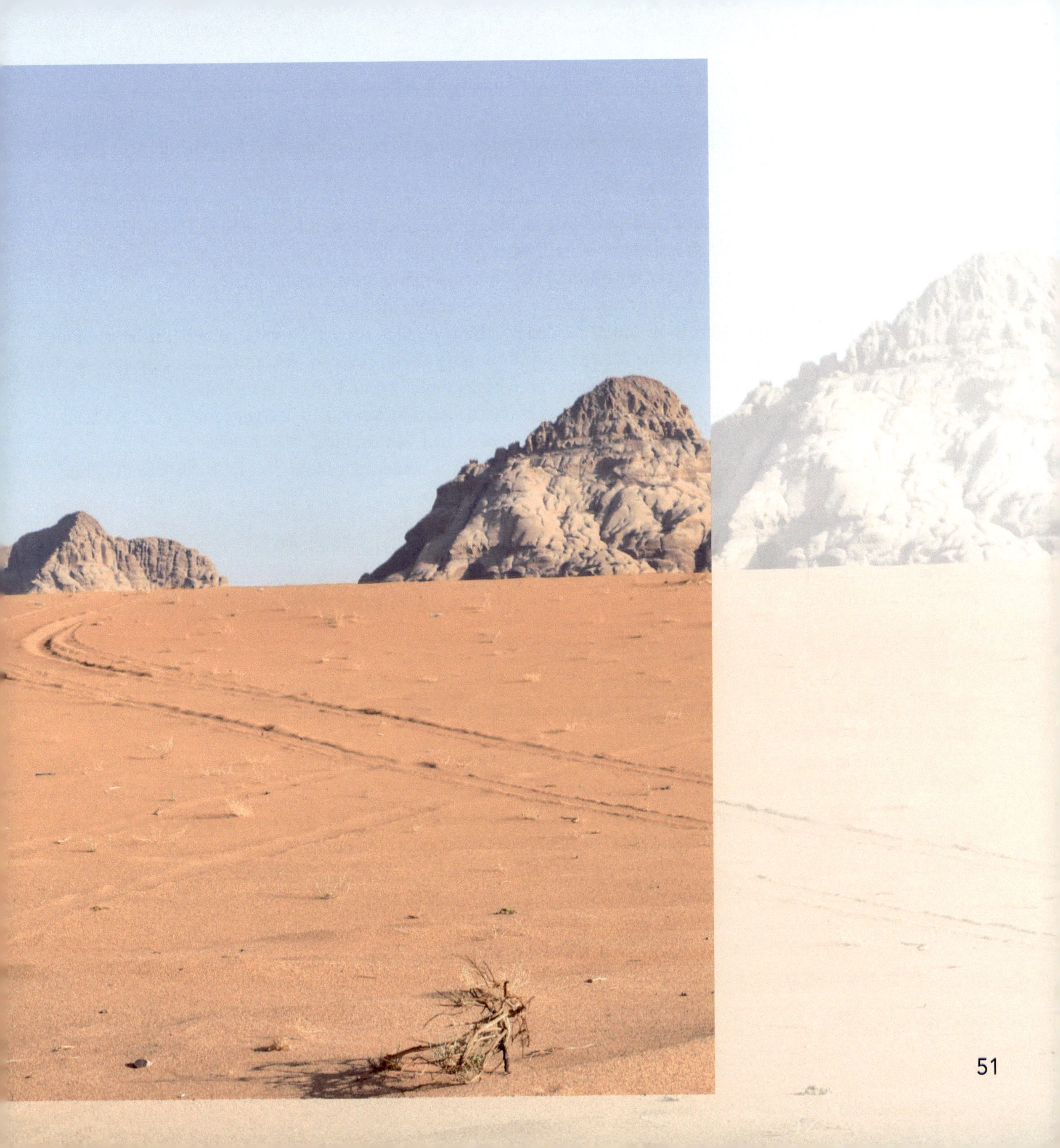

the sunbathers for food, while Leo remained in the water dipping under every once in a while but mostly just floating on its surface.

"If you think about it, this is probably the first time he's gotten to relax in months," Max mentioned, as they all watched him float in his own world.

"Shit, yeah, I didn't think about that," Daphne said.

"Yeah, his dad's been a total dick about college decisions. Like getting into Brown is fucking easy. He literally got into Cornell and UChicago and his dad's still disappointed," Max explained.

"Wish I could give him a piece of my mind," Margot furrowed her brow, frowning.

"Don't we all," Astrid sighed, throwing a pebble next to her into the water.

"I'm glad we did this guys. He obviously needed it, I think we all needed it. I hope it helped him let go of his dad's voice in his head," Daphne resolved, standing up and running off the boulder. "Incoming!" she screamed, as she cannonballed into the water next to Leo. She swam over to him, grabbing onto him to stay afloat.

"Hey," Leo smiled, but his lips were purple and his teeth were chattering and Margot could no longer make out that flush he always got with Daphne. Instead his skin looked pale, almost blue.

"Leo you don't look okay, oh my god you're frozen," Daphne panicked, calling the group down to drag him out of the water to a combined blanket of everyone's towels.

"I'm fine guys, don't even worry," Leo said through a gritted smile.

"You're definitely not, we need to find a campsite now and get you near a fire," Astrid said, face strained, hand feeling his cold cheek. With one arm around Max and the other around Astrid, Leo was carried through the last of the trail that led to a cleared campsite about a mile from the watering hole. Daphne built his tent for him while Margot
started up a fire.

As he sat by the small fire while the rest of the group collected sticks, Margot watched him scrunch his eyes, drop his head, and cry into his hands. She knew he wasn't crying because he was sick. She sat on the rock next to him, throwing twigs onto the flame.

"I don't know you as the kind of person to cry over the cold, so what's up?" Margot asked gently, facing the fire. He stayed silent for a moment, sniffling, gathering his thoughts.

"You all helped me immediately, no questions asked," Leo smiled through his tears. "You didn't call me weak, or stupid for staying in too long. You just gave me all of your towels and your care and … I love you guys so much, how did I get so lucky?"

"Oh my gosh, Leo. You didn't get lucky, we're friends because you bring out the best in us," Margot smiled, tears brimming in her own eyes, touched by this gratitude. She knew that his father would have done differently. Hell, he might've left him to take care of himself, shivering and sick.

"I'm scared of saying no to him, but I want you to know how much better I've gotten. I fought so hard for this trip, because y'all inspire me. If I could have it my way, we'd all stay up here together, away from the world and its evil fathers forever," he laughed, dropping his head.

"You know we'd all love that," Margot pushed his knee playfully and nodded her head toward the clearing of the campsite. Daphne sat at the edge of the opening of one of the tents she had set up, reading a book.

"I didn't think you knew," Leo's face flushed a hard red in the firelight.

"The only one who doesn't is her," Margot gave him a grin. He smiled back.

"I don't think I'm good enough for her," he quietly admitted, holding his hands up to the fire to warm them.

"How so?"

"She's so unrestricted with her creativity and caring and emotion. She has an insatiable drive for life and her passions I'm so impressed by. She is so confident it strikes me dead every time I watch her walk into a room knowing she's going to make it better. Her smile is contagious, she makes me so nervous and she doesn't even realize it," His eyes were sparkling with the flames of the fire as he spoke, eyes darting from her to the conversation and back.

"And you? You are understanding and brave and determined. If it doesn't work out the way you'd like, there's no harm in staying friends. All I ask is that you are careful. Daphne deserves the absolute best from you. If you're not in a state to devote your time and energy to making her days sunnier, I'd tell you to back off," Margot warned.

"You're right. I think I need to wait," he agreed solemnly.

"That doesn't mean you can't go over there and ask her about that book right now," Margot smirked. Leo laughed and smiled.

"Thank you, Marg. I promise to follow your advice," he said, sniffling from his sickness as he got up and headed over to Daphne's silhouette in the dawn light. And Margot knew he would. There were certain men in the world she felt were taught a gentleness that she trusted. A gentleness Leo carried. He was the opposite of his father, on purpose she supposed, and she loved him for it. She joined Max and Astrid in setting up the second tent.

The wind had picked up its pace as the night aged, its gusts howling outside of the small, green tent. Margot laid at the edge of her tent facing its walls, Max in the center, and Leo shivering on the other side. Leo's ears were covered by Astrid's hat and he was tucked beneath both a sleeping bag and a make-shift blanket of everyone's down coats. Margot, on the other hand, could feel her sweat gathering in a sheet atop her skin, overheating in the close quarters. She could feel the sleeping bag latch to her damp skin, the hairs at the nape of her neck curl, and, surprisingly, Max's eyes burning into the back of her skull. Leo's snoring, deep asleep in his sickness, was the only sound she could make out above the wind. She knew Max was never good at falling asleep and she knew Max was silently awake now, as if waiting for her to turn around, to relieve him of his patience.

His eyes burned deeper and deeper, and the wind howled louder, and the droplet of sweat dripping down her forehead slid painstakingly slowly until it suddenly dripped into her eye and she had had enough. She turned over abruptly and stared him straight in the eyes, brown irises meeting brown irises. Max stayed quiet, his mouth only dropping slightly agape, words lost to him.

"Ask," was all Margot could stutter out, his continued silence shocking her. She didn't even know if it was a question that he wished to verbalize.

As if on schedule the wind whistled a powerful flow of air through the tent, bringing Max to his senses. He bowed his head, then raised his eyes once again.

"Aren't you scared?" he questioned softly.

Rachel Pellom '24

Amelia Fay '25

"Of what?"

"Of losing this."

"Losing what?"

"Us. I mean, I'm moving half way across the fucking country and the closest I'll be to any of you is a ten-hour drive at least. I mean, fuck Margot, you're a month's paycheck of a plane ride away." Here, Margot could make out the real reason Max couldn't sleep. She brought a hand up to his cheek and there they were. Tears.

One thing about Max Rowe was that he never cried. This was not to say that he avoided emotion altogether. No, in fact he embraced it. If he was happy, you could tell by his wide smiles and his small laughs to himself. If he was sad, he would refuse to look you in your eyes, and hang his head, but never refuse a hug. All of the emotions in between he expressed fully. But in her eighteen years of knowing him, never once had she watched a tear well in his eye.

There is something uniquely melancholy about knowing exactly the type of despair someone else is feeling. Feeling him cry then, in the wind-besieged tent, on the last Friday of summer, over her, over them, over this loss they were all bracing for, made her throat sting and her cheeks flush and quieted the gusts and the snoring and left her only with the feeling of her hand on his cheek wiping those tears as if to wipe all of theirs.

"Turn on the lamp," she whispered, eyes still on him, hand still on him. He did as she asked, flicking on the yellow light of the battery-powered lamp laid between them. She could see his red eyes more clearly now, and he hers, she assumed. His chin trembled in the same way the wind shook the tent, refusing to rest.

"I want to turn it off, it's too much I —" his voice shook as she looked at him in the light.

"Please," she grabbed his hand, "let me draw you." His eyebrows softened at this. He closed his eyes and breathed into his decision.

"Ok," he resolved.

She fumbled around on her side of the tent and shortly Margot had flipped open a well-used sketchbook to a blank page. She ran her hand over the page, a step she never left out, and then looked at Max's face. First, his face structure. His jaw was square, her pencil etching his angular edges and then his wide neck. His ears were next, slim against the sides of his head. Then, his eyebrows. Margot began with light, hair-like strokes at their fronts, then pressing harder and harder into the parchment as they thinned out to the edges.

When she reached his eyes, she didn't even need to look back up at his stoic face. She knew these eyes like she knew how her father liked his toast and every twist and turn of the path to the river's beach. She looked at these eyes in the mirror every morning because, in some unexplainable way, Max and Margot shared the same eyes. Dark, penetrating lashes, deep brown irises punctuated by black holes, all sunken into the face within the faintest rings of purple. Even with the same eyes, Margot always envied the way his nose rose from their canyons, a perfect, structured mountain. From his sharp nose to his pointed lips, Margot's pencil brought him out of the paper exactly as he was right then.

As she was finishing the dark, messy curls atop his head, she felt something gentle touch her face. A hand, his hand, his thumb swiping across her cheek. And eyes flickering up to his, she finally realized she was crying, throat sore, as she drew her friend for the first and last time.

"You know me so well," he was looking at the drawing now, referring to the realism of the image that could only be the result of years spent together. His eyes were red with a sorrow Margot could feel in herself. All she could do was grab him and pull him into a hug.

She did know him well. Four years felt like decades between her loud soul and his quiet one. Margot rubbed his back and pulled away, tearing the drawing from her sketchbook handing it to him.

"You're not losing us. We'll just be farther away," she smiled.

"I'm not losing you… I won't lose this," he sniffled, getting up, unzipping the tent, and heading for his backpack leaned against a nearby tree. But the wind had grown fierce as the night had progressed: its gusts whipped Max's dark curls back and forth, and the drawing right out of his hand. The paper twirled and fluttered into the collection of trees just beside the campgrounds. "No. Fuck! Margot I'm so sorry … I didn't mean to."

Margot could see the distress in his eyes. It was obvious the drawing meant a lot to him and she desperately wanted him to have it.

"It's ok, I'm going to find it. Stay here, try to get some sleep," Margot said over her shoulder, maneuvering out of the tent and heading towards where the paper flew. Margot could not explain why her fear of the dark and unknown evaded her that night, but she forged forward into the abyss of forest.

Margot couldn't see her feet ahead of her as she stumbled through the trees, eyes peeled for the bright white of the paper. Her hair and clothes billowed about her, the wind rushing over her face, stomach and legs giving her a chill. She moved from tree to tree, grasping onto their trunks for stability. After a couple minutes of searching, a bright spot appeared several yards ahead of her. Excited, Margot rushed towards it, but as she moved closer, it became larger and larger and soon she realized she had reached a clearing.

She ground to a stop, stunned by the view before her. The ground below her tapered off into a cliff and the moon was glowing white above a landscape of indescribable impact ahead of it. Mountains rising from the earth as if being pulled up by the moon itself, valleys glowing with the dots of lampposts and late-night wakers.

The vastness of the scene made Margot feel small. Not insignificant, but the feeling of being a child beneath skyscrapers in comparison to the breadth and history of the earth around her now. The mountains commanded the skyline, the moon rose as she knew it had for as long as she could imagine. People had seen these same mountains, this same moon, and felt this same wind hundreds of thousands of years before her. But something she couldn't let go of was the feeling of honor that came with knowing that she was interconnected with these strong mountains and beautiful moon and peaceful valleys and histories of human and terrain.

"Margot! Margot, are you okay? Margot!" a voice rang out over the wind. Max's flashlight shone through the gaps between the trees, snapping her out of her epiphany and beckoning her back. Margot stayed a second more with this intense feeling of comfort, and called back.

"I'm here, don't worry! I'm coming to you!"

Max walked her back to the camp, flashlight guiding their steps. She felt the regret of having not found the paper, but a swell of gratitude to simply be sharing the night with the trees and the ground and one of the people she loved most in the world came over her.

In the tent, she was comforted by the warmth of Max sleeping beside her. She was not as scared now, to come down from this mountain and face her future, and this peace put her to sleep.

⛺ continued on page 136 ⛺

Amelia Fay '25

greed and guts
Anonymous

Everything moves,
but I do not move with them.
Observation is my game.
I see those who cut me down,
I see the houses built of me
from the backyards that they
so meticulously,
systematically,
removed my bodies from.
Trying to tame something that does not need to be tamed.
I live for as long as it is convenient for them.
I give them oxygen,
and in exchange,
I get pruning.
I see the games that they play
with the creatures that run through my forests.
Always the same side loses.
The doe never wins.
Guns
that are people
that say
"protection"
"safety"
as red flowers bloom.
Aesthetic and sport and sustenance.
I am not all for them.

Let the wild things be wild.

Catherine Gao '24

Rachel Pellom '24

Katelyn Miller '24

guests who (couldn't) stay

Kiersten Hackman '24

imagine a world bursting at the seams
with greens—and the c r a w l
up your spine
feels familiar
like maybe your nerves have always grown
from this damp earth
spinning, tipsy on cheap mint julep
served best: stale on a chipped platter
(the hotel logo embossed
beneath the moist ring left by the glass).
now—wrap your fingers around this
Room of Temporary
edged by peeling layers of paint, their
sickly scent long drunken up
by the fleeting past,
guests who stay: for rest, for pleasure
for necessity, for weeping—it matters not
to the pasty lark green walls
resigned to witnessing in silence.

Catherine Gao '24

Olivia Rivers '24

the nut and the tree

Hannah Elman '27

The nut falls from the tree,
The fall long and treacherous,
Before reaching the cold, hard ground.

The nut knows not what to be,
It just is.

The nut has left the safety and comfort of the tree,
Not by choice,
But by will.

The nut knows not how to be frightened,
It just is.

And soon, perhaps a squirrel will come,
And take the nut,
Far, far away

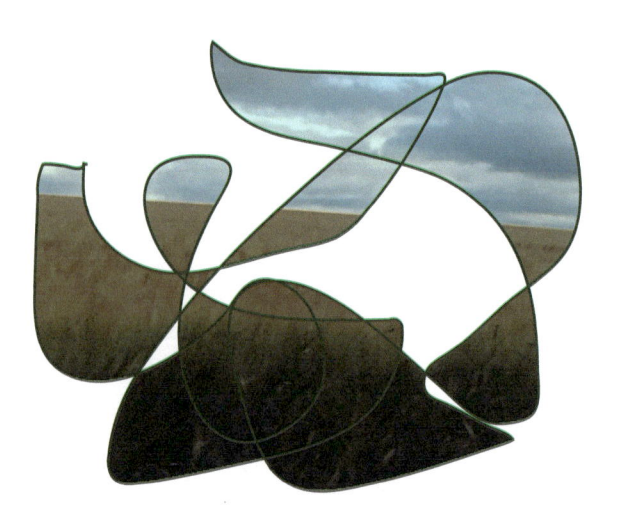

And perhaps,
On the way to far, far away,
The nut will fall out of the squirrel's grasp,
Plummeting to the ground again,
As the squirrel runs along,
Into a distant and unknown forest.

Perhaps.

And perhaps, the nut will fall,
So, so far
It will burrow into the ground,
Deep into the cold soil.

And, perhaps it will sprout roots,
Big and sturdy and strong.

Then, perhaps, nut nut will start to grow,
First into a sapling,
Then a young tree,
Then finally into a huge, tall tree,
Big and sturdy and strong.

Amelia Fay '25

And, perhaps, the tree will end up growing nuts of its own,
Which will fall and start the cycle anew.

But that's just a thought,
It's really up to you;
So which one will you be,
A tree, or something new.

"daydream," *Catherine Gao '24*

Milo King '24

the death of me

Anonymous

I am sick and empty.
I wish you would pull the plug.

You are mentally ill and obsessive.
I am mentally ill and obsessive.
But you were sweet and kind,
And I was willing and able.

The incense and the knives.
And the knives are my fault.
The music is my fault
It's all my fault.
Is it my fault?

Pull the plug.

"I wouldn't trade you for anything"
You traded me for everything.

You're a dog
I'm a dog.
We're dogs.
I bet on losing dogs.

Pull the plug.

You write and you dream and you talk
And I listen.
And it's my fault.
It's my fault?

You punch yourself in the face.
And it's my fault.
Is it my fault?
Why is it my fault?
I am not your hands.

Pull the plug.

"With insurmountable love"
You never loved me.
If you loved me you would

Pull the plug.

"I'll always be your friend as long as you want me around"
You left.

Pull the plug before you leave.

I felt wanted.
WANTED.
I was blind.
BLIND.

"I want to be able to help you get better"
I wanted you to get better.
You need my love
I couldn't love you how you wanted me to.

Pull the plug.
Please.

They all see me now
They all hate me now.
I'm sick and twisted.
They see too much of me.

Why didn't you just pull the plug?

So this is my legacy.
You have turned me into a monster for them to
Point and laugh

And I just stand in my transparent box
With all the gaping mouths and painful eyes
The eyes are all around they don't leave they never leave.
They're always watching.
I'm deformed.
You made me this way.

I bite the hand that feeds me.
You fed me lies.
I bit your hand.

Pull the plug.
Watch me die.
I need you to watch me die.
To watch me shrivel and pale.
This is my fault.
This is your fault.

Pull the plug.

Rachel Pellom '24

the long walk home
Katelyn Miller '24

i take nostalgia pills each morning to
forget who i am.
not to remember the past
because the past is the past
and the present is a "present"
but to forget the
barbed wires that stick through
the thin paper of my future.

each day the pill becomes a little less
potent and I — a little more tired.
as the barbed wires wrap circles around
my arms
pulling me down, deeper
it's darker here.

it's only when
i hear the birds chirping
the same way they always did,
and the neighbor's dog barks
just as obnoxiously as the day before,

that the walk up my steep driveway becomes
a little less daunting.

Rachel Pellom '24

Catherine Gao '24

Kilian Sadowski de Prada '25

the ocean must remain still

Katelyn Miller '24

    The woman was an actress. She was a performer. She didn't have a name and didn't need one. She was only known by her all too tempting curves and all too obnoxious voice. Yet, despite her irregularities, her brashness, her boldness, she still brought in business. Mainly because, despite her immensity, she was still a spectacle trapped in the cage, like a tiger in a circus. She was strong and powerful, but reduced to something to watch and laugh at. Her talents were exhibited around the world in front of politicians, kings, and princes. Over time, she had learned to tone down her unpleasantly high-pitched laugh and echoing voice in order to be who they wanted. All of the men would come to watch, because she was the best at her job. I'm an entertainer. *I chose this life.*

    She remembers being in second grade and loving jellyfish, never understanding why everyone was so afraid of them. They just floated around in the ocean, minding their own, and if some unfortunate soul was unlucky enough to be hit by their sting, that wasn't the jellyfish's fault. In fact, she always thought people should stay out of the water in the first place. To let the wild things remain wild. Yet, people seemed to have a tendency to try to control what they can't. She learned *that* in second grade when she pulled Johnny's pants down after he made a mean face at her. She knew she shouldn't have. She knew it was wrong, but it was awfully funny. The most vivid moment of the experience was when she complained to her best friend Alice, "How come *I* get in trouble when I do that, but when Johnny does it to other boys the teachers just laugh!"

    "That's just how it is," Alice rolled her eyes.

So, she learned that the world controls the brash and the loud; they controlled her simply because she was too *much*.

    As time went on, and the world continued to push her down, to kick and scratch and force her into a box, she became all the more subdued. Her parents would say, "When are you going to get a job? When are you going to contribute to the world?" So she tried and tried and tried, but each place she went had a different reason to deny her. *You're too abrasive.* She had only been trying to be bold. *You might be a little too forward for our audience.* She had only spoken the truth. *You don't really fit what we're looking for.* She had only worn what made her comfortable.

    "The world only likes women when they're small," she told her best friend after the tenth consecutive rejection from an interview. "And I'm 5'11 and 180 pounds and deemed too large for a woman in all ways possible it seems." When she told others "Mother Earth is 13,170,000,000,000,000,000,000,000 pounds large and 8000 miles tall and we still love her," people would laugh. It wasn't until she was a few years older that she realized we don't love Mother Earth either. The more she tried to fight this invisible force, the more she felt like she was drowning.

Yet, one day that she remembers as vividly as the sun on a cloudy day, she was told yes. In a dark brick building, with flickering lights and the screeching of metal chairs across the cold concrete floor, she was told yes. "I think you would make a great addition to our acting company. In fact, I think you could be a real star here." The world tilted on its axis and the planet spun out of orbit because she felt *wanted*. Grabbing the contract like it was a worthless paper towel, she skipped to the last page and signed her name, bolded and in red: permanent. The marker leaked through the page, making stains on the table and leaving behind her legacy. As she walked home, she thought about how excited she was to tell her parents all that she had accomplished.

"You'll have to live in the acting compound to prepare for our shows," the man had said. "I'll give you a few days to pick up your life and move here."

I've finally made it.

A few days later, she walked through the neighborhood she had grown up in, passing by her elementary school. Children's laughs rang out from the courtyard as the bell rang for recess to begin. She smiled, thinking about how happy she had been when she was their age. *I fear the day that life hits them in the face.* The wind picked up, causing her hair to lift behind her, as she continued her walk towards her new future.

At first it was good. People with deep sunken eyes brought her food and coffee everyday. She had unnamed helpers do her hair, her makeup, and hand sew her outfits. The man kept telling her, "You're the new prodigy of the company!" Everyday, she would walk through hallways plastered with her face, not noticing that her name was always missing from the posters.

But as time went on and the days shortened and darkened into winter, she darkened along with them. The sunken eyes of her helpers became those of her own. The plays she put on were crude and unusual, full of sex and drugs and things she didn't believe in. She found herself no longer believing in God because if God was real why would he put her in such a place? Why would he allow her to not read the contract that says, in small print, "We own the rights to your face and your body." *But it's MY body and My face!* From then on she was known as the nameless actress who brought an audience from around the world, but couldn't look herself in the mirror. She had taped it up so she couldn't see what she had become. The man kept picking at her skin, telling her to be thinner but curvy, louder but quiet. If she wanted to talk on the phone, she was monitored, so she had to grin and lie through her teeth, "I'm doing great, Mom!" No one tells you that when you sell your body for fame, your soul goes along with it.

The void that filled her deepened and blackened until it almost covered her completely. Until she snapped.

She doesn't remember exactly what happened, only clenching her fists and blacking out until her hands were soaked with blood and her fingernails were full of flesh. Until she had the man's face in her hands. *He stole my face, I just did the same thing back. There's nothing wrong with that. There's nothing wrong with that. There's nothing wrong with me.* She ran. She stole his face and ran and ran and ran until her heart was pounding and she couldn't run anymore. When she finally looked up, she saw she had come to her elementary school. It was night and the children were gone, but she pictured herself sitting on swings and chewing mulch between her teeth. She imagined running around, free and untethered by the constraints she now faced; so she did.

The grass left large stains on her vulgar shirt as she tumbled through the playground, pretending she was free and her time wasn't up. Making her way into the building, she stumbled into the bathroom she had cried in after being told she was getting suspended for pulling Johnny's pants down. The mirror here wasn't taped up like the one at the compound and she could finally see the monster she had become.

    Sirens blared all around, the building was surrounded and she felt heat rise to her face. *What have I done?* But her reflection just stared back. It seemed otherworldly. It was as if a ghost had taken control of her body and she was watching all of this happen from the outside. The sirens were too loud and soon it would be over. *It will be over.* The more she looked at her twin on the other side, the more she clenched her fists. Her nails dug deep scars into her palms as she continued to look. The figure just observed her and the more she looked back, the more it began to change. It shrank, becoming thinner and shorter. Her loud blushing cheeks became soft and simple. Her big hair and crooked teeth were both straightened. She was small enough to be untouched. As she reached out her hand, trying to grab this unattainable version of herself, she was stopped by the cold glass of reality. Her time was up. She had been found. She had made too many waves in a sea that only wanted to remain calm and unchanged. ♛

Mai Malesky '25

Amelia Fay '25

hell in a handbasket

Taylor Winstead '24

the worst feeling isn't going to hell
it's going to hell again
I went there in a handbasket made it halfway back and fell down again
down a rabbit hole whose
walls I knew like the dirt caked palm of my hand

it's glimpsing God and then knowing you'll never have him
a foot and a half through the gate then turned away
halfway over the fence when it snatches me back

hell doesn't burn
it freezes

hell doesn't shriek
it goes silent and everyone averts their eyes

hell doesn't gnash its teeth
we keep our mouths closed

hell doesn't tempt
we follow it willingly

medium

John McGowan '24

    I am a liar and this is my confession. More specifically, I am a medium. My clients believe I can talk to dead people. This is not true. I tell them I can talk to dead people and they pay me to "talk" to their loved ones. Of all the professions I have practiced, medium is the only one I can justify. I used to be a run of the mill conman. I scammed people out of their money. Usually, I scammed people who needed money the most but were too stupid or too nice to hold on to what little they had. A lot of conmen like to pretend they only targeted the rich or greedy. I know for a fact this is not true. The rich and the greedy are far more difficult to steal from because they are so intent on not losing what they have that they don't trust anyone to handle their money. And that's how most scams operate, in order to con someone out of their money, you first have to get a hold of it, which requires them to trust you. I would go so far as to say that trust is the most profitable and important commodity our society deals with. My clients trust me to be an accurate messenger beyond the veil. Whether or not this trust is misplaced is irrelevant. To my clients, my powers are real, and that's all that matters. I'm not just taking money from grieving families and leaving them with nothing but more loss, I'm comforting them. So they're not paying me to speak with dead people, they're paying me to comfort them about their loss. I mean, when you get down to it, how different am I from the preacher who gets paid to say their loved one went to heaven and is smiling down with angels and Jesus and all the other people they loved who died. Isn't the preacher lying too? **If hell is real then some preachers have to have lied at some point, because not everyone goes to heaven.** And I've never heard a preacher say, "Whelp, your Grandpa's probably down there shoveling shit with Satan, so don't worry, he's getting what he deserved."

    That's how I sleep at night.

    I've always been good at lying. I can't remember the first time I lied. It was probably to my mother or father, and I probably lied about something stupid, like stealing sweets. I can remember the first time I scammed someone. I think I was seven or eight and Susie was selling Girlscout cookies at school. They were three bucks a box and every other kid in my class had cash from their parents to buy cookies but me. I had a quarter I had found laying on the bathroom floor that morning. When it was my turn to buy cookies, I told her the quarter was special because it had ridges instead of smooth sides and that really it was far more valuable than three dollars but because I was feeling generous I would be willing to trade it for a box of cookies. She was too young to know what bullshit smelled like. From there, my career began.

Rachel Pellom '24

    I became a medium after I realized that it was a far more reliable source of income than running scams on the street. It was also legally sanctioned. I could lie without ever getting in trouble. I learned quickly that the trick to speaking to the dead is to say things that are sort of opposite, that way, you cover all your bases. The client just picks up on what they want to hear and ignores the rest. For example, I told a man his dead mother "wanted him to feel secure and safe and not take too many risks" but that she also "wanted him to express his freedom, step out of his comfort zone and try new things." Sort of opposites. Apparently, he only heard the second part of my reading, because he told me he was looking for a sign to repaint his bathroom a bright shade of orange. He showed me pictures after the job was complete. It was horrid and gauche. I told him it's what his mother would have wanted. He gave me six hundred dollars.

    He was a regular client, so I didn't have to work very hard to get him to trust me. He already bought my lies hook, line, and sinker. The real challenge of being a medium is winning over new customers. Sometimes they're just skeptics looking to prove me wrong. They usually do and at the end of the session stand up and proudly proclaim they have caught me in a lie. I have developed a very formulaic response to these individuals, and it works everytime. When they say, "You liar, my father would never say that, I have caught you! What do you have to say for yourself?" I simply ask, "Cash or card?"

A Baby Camel in Wadi Rum, *Rachel Pellom '24*

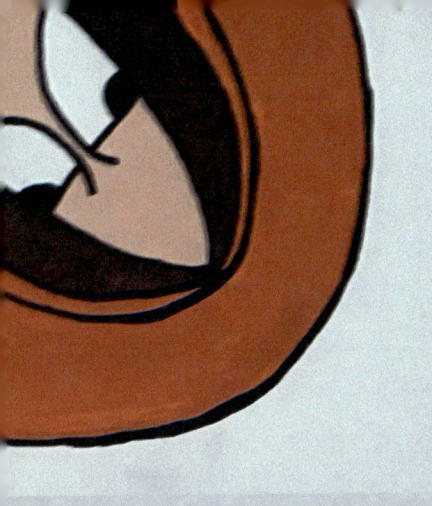

i ate augustus

Blake Roper '24

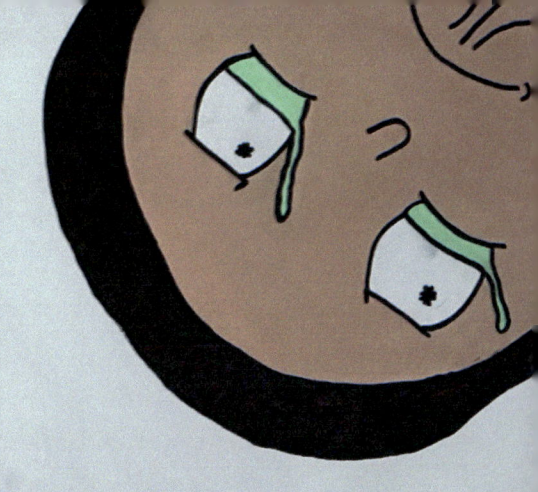

In history class I was very sad

For I had just learned something very bad

In 410 they looted his grave

And his ashes, no one could save

Scattered on Italian ground

In a field with scarcely-a-sound

Maybe in a field of wheat

Swaying in the summer heat

Now I can't get it out of my head

That a bit of Augustus could be in my bread.

Anderson Levin '26

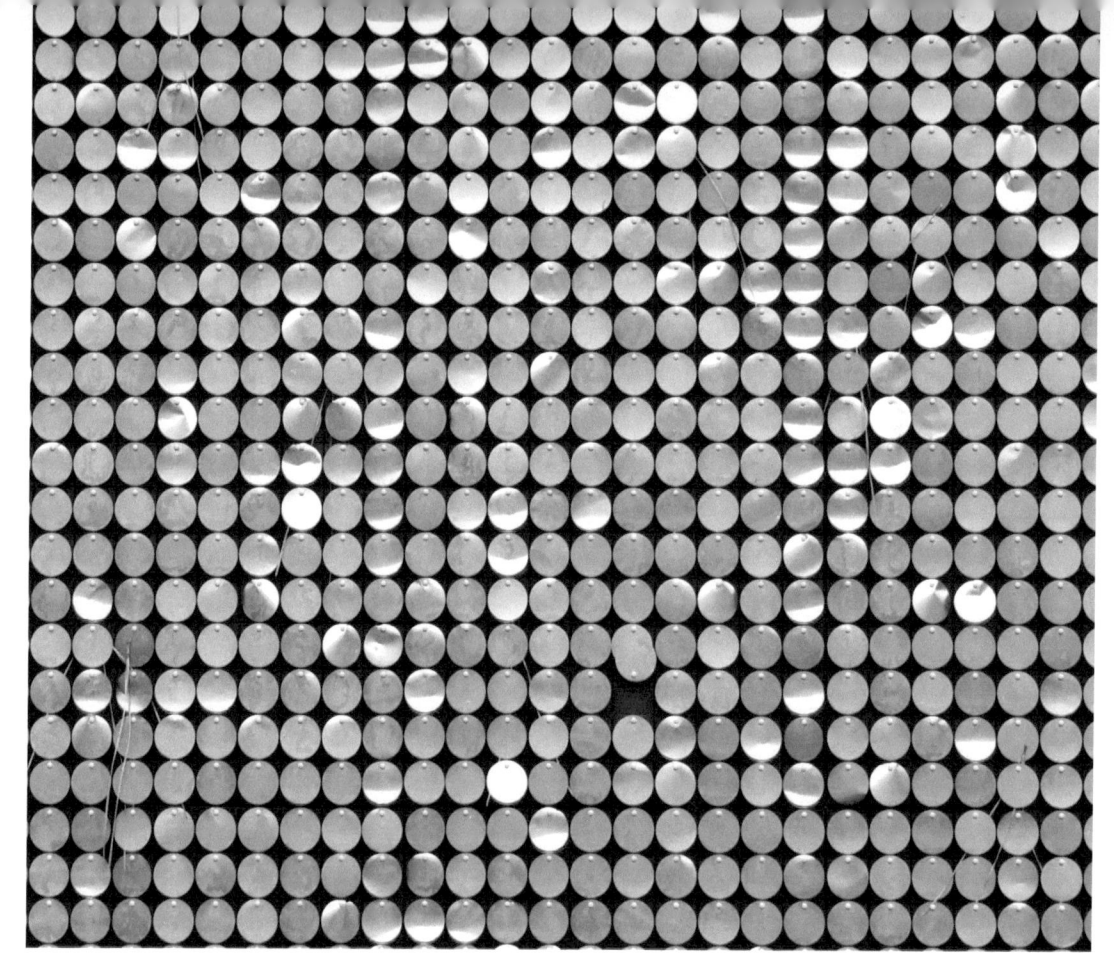

Rachel Pellom '24

canción primavera

Tony Varela '26

Invierno se
Va; invita de vuelta
Su canto dulce.

fire escape

Azif

She is a living flame.
In her flickers I see
Aeons of civilization swallowed by a rising sun and spat out on the balance of a needle.
Oil belching motoroids stroking the fogged glass, resting their sadness on an elbow.
A dark stage centering a world on fire, and an audience of blank and staring faces.
I see the shrieking, bloody, sister-raping beast from which I came and the chrome-wired posthuman I am to be.
Evenings, mornings, afternoons to sit around and wonder what to do with your time.
Time to criticize yourself and pedestal your idols.
Time to bring back dead conversations just to kill them once again.
Time to ascend the darkened stair and be quietly devoured.
Time to scramble through the rocks in search of an entirely different mind.
Time to readjust your chair and place a finger on your chin.
Time to let your thoughts die and
Time to look into her eyes and have a quiet renaissance.
That's all I want with her.
Time.

The Death of Math

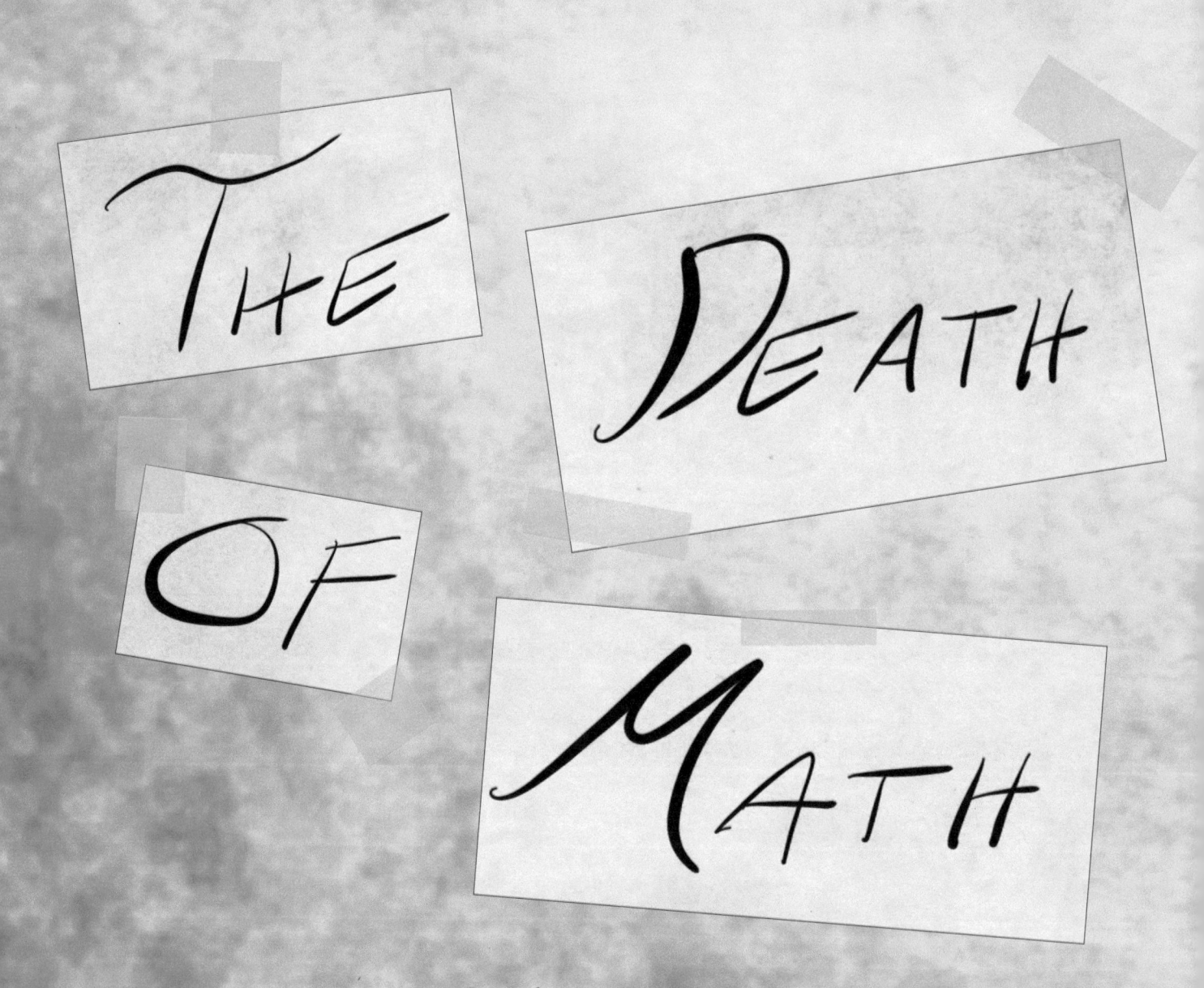

Dr. Andrew Prudhom, Faculty

1. Horses

Do you know the story of the Equinian Tragedy? The horse was a dear friend to humanity. It has the peculiar distinction of being one of the few terrestrial creatures to circumnavigate the globe, although that is a journey we made together.

Horses evolved on the plains of North America before the last major ice age. When the great glaciers locking off the northern tundra receded, horses followed. They eventually made their way to northeastern Asia during a period of remarkably low tides.

On those foreign planes, horses had a chance meeting that forever changed their fate. A quick partnership with humanity, and suddenly horses were half of the most powerful invention of its age — horseback archers. Mongols used them to great effect, and spread horses and husbandry techniques through the entirety of their known world. Arabian cultures spread them further, until horses were synonymous with humanity.

Rachel Pellom '24

Prisoner, Sophie Williamson '27

Eventually, horses traversed the ocean in repurposed trees lashed together by their sapian companions, and returned to their ancestral home. Unbeknownst to the Eurasian population, the American horse had gone extinct long before, and the modern horse found a landscape begging for its presence. They quickly went wild, establishing the wild horse populations we see today.

This tight partnership between horse and man endured for eons, and ended in an instant. Within two generations of the invention of the modern combustion engine and the automobile, horses went from an everyday companion species — a species that lived with us in our towns, like dogs and cats do today, to a passing rarity. There was a time where anyone of modest means had a horse. Within 100 years, no one had a horse. What happened to all the horses?

Therein lies the central question of the Equinian Tragedy. How did this essential companion creature vanish from our lives? And what else are we sacrificing on the altar of progress?

11. GEARS

Have you heard of the Antikithera Mechanism? It is a fascinating story. Around the turn of the 20th century, a sunken ship off the coast of Greece (near the place known as Antikithera) yielded an artifact most mysterious. Around the size of a laptop, the mechanism appeared to be a metal block, but obviously worked by intelligence.

Modern scanning techniques reveal a masterwork of intricately composed gears fill the mechanism. Precision engineered, the artistry of the mechanism's construction may well be unrivaled in modern times. The knowledge of gear systems as complex as the Antikithera Mechanism's exists in written form, but the number of living humans capable of comprehending the mechanism is likely numbered in the dozens, if that.

This does not mean that the inventor of the Antikithera Mechanism was "smarter" than modern scholars. It is simply a fact that the best minds of modern times live in a world of transistors and electric motors. The art of transferring a motive force through a gear system, so motion in one place causes motion precisely elsewhere, is not a living art in modern humanity.

Amelia Fay '25

For centuries, the concept of gear systems had a very fruitful partnership with humanity. Societies that understood how to channel physical force through a system of gears outperformed those who didn't just as readily as societies who had partnered with horses replaced those that did not. But, within a generation or two of the invention of the transister and digital circlentry, the taming of lightning, repurposed from mythical mystery to beast of burden, and knowledge of gears had largely vanished. Yes, the knowledge was recorded, but it no longer lived in the minds of its simian champions.

In studying the Antikithera Mechanism, modern scholars are rediscovering incredible ingenuities concerning gears. We don't know who built the mechanism, but whoever it was one thing is clear: they were an absolute master of their craft. How did gears go from such an essential companion concept in ancient times to an eccentricity in modern times? Can the equinian tragedy befall an idea? And if it can, what else is at risk of inadvertant sacrifice on the altar of progress?

Olivia Rivers '24

90

Amelia Fay '25

III. Mathematics

The love story between math and minds is one of the greatest in our species' history. The two are so intertwined that even the fundamental distinction between them is nebulous. Did our minds invent the intricacies of mathematics, or did the structure of mathematics scaffold our minds? At some point in the distant past, humanity began to deeply ponder mathematics, and forever altered its future.

Societies that allowed mathematics into their minds could build better bridges, plan more successful wars, more accurately ration crops through winter, make more useful maps, and administrate larger empires. For eons, the study of mathematics made humanity possible. Young children were taught math to train their brains in the art of reason. Hundreds, thousands, millions of humans underwent rigorous training in the artform, becoming the literal engineers of humanity's progress.

This great partnership between concept and creature lasted for eons, and ended in an instant. Within two generations of the invention of artificial intelligence, no one was being trained as a computer scientist, none but the most privileged were being shown the wonders of our oldest partnership.

In the age of A.I., mathematics has found fertile augar in the silicon mind of the machine. No longer must a human engineer design a bridge, just upload the specifics of the scenario and an A.I. can make a better bridge in a fraction of the time. Blueprints no longer require a human architect with knowledge of stress & shear, an algorithm can design better, with less energy consumption and less waste material, too.

Mathematics was our greatest strength and our most powerful tool, but in the modern day it is a tool more fit for minds of circuits than those of synapse. But, what does this mean? If math is no longer a tool of man, what is it?

I propose that it is what it has always been: a toy. An intellectual curiosity without purpose, math at its heart is simply indulging in ungoverned speculation for the sake of the marvellous. Do not let math go the way of horses. Perhaps it would be better described as a Perilavssean tragedy, as we are being sacrificed on an altar of our own design, but the death of mathematics would be the equenian tragedy of our age. Before it is too late, we must remember: math is a toy, not a tool.

Margaret Jester '24

Amelia Fay '25

94

Margaret Jester '24

i am a tree

Chloe Bidgood '25

I am a tree

Dogs shit on me

Pomeranians and poodles

Dobermans and doodles

They all shit on me

And if you don't clean it

I'll make you eat it

Hiking on an autumn day, colorful leaves crunching beneath your boot

Too bad you didn't see my root

Tumbling forwards, bracing yourself for the fall

Oh, this is just a ball!

Face first in your dog's creation

Not cleaning it up was your own invitation

I chuckle bitterly

You ate shit literally

I do too much for you

You ate shit, boo-hoo

Without me this planet would undoubtedly be in flames

You humans and your stupid planes

You all should be copying the Lorax

Instead, you spend your time searching up "slime with no borax"

Get up you little wretches

Maybe go outside and do some stretches

Touch grass, you little lass

I'm an old tree

I've been around longer than you can see

Not one of you will outlast me

The gas stations, the schools and the Cook Outs

Oh, you better watch out

I stand tall in this world

The one that belongs to me, my world

You can cut me down

But you'll never make me frown

I may not be The Giving Tree

They were far too compassionate for me

But I am mother nature's pride

And I take it in stride

You may never clean up after your pets

But not to fret

I won't take shit from anyone, dog, bear, or bee

"Greedy Birds", *Ashley Slomianyj '26*

Olivia Rivers '24

"Lego Charcoal Flower", *Ashley Slomianyj '26*

Amelia Fay '25

scarab

Katelyn Miller '24

the tires of my car leave
    claw marks in the grass.

they're muddy and deep
    and too wide and too noticeable.

my father tells me to stop messing up our
    lawn. *the neighbors will see.*

yet, I run over the same little patch
    unable to avoid the delicate tendrils.

my mother doesn't seem to notice.
    too busy with the books and the boredom and the beetles.

the beetles, the beetles, *Popillia japonica*
    devouring our beautiful Crimson Queen.

so my father gets mad at me and the bugs
    am I just a japanese beetle?

disruptive, invasive, pervasive,
    always out of place.

when I use my four year old Macbook to look them up,
    Google assumes they are my mortal enemy.

he tells me People also ask:
    What kills Japanese Beetles the best?

Will Japanese Beetles go away on their own?
    How do you control Japanese Beetles?

And although I didn't ask,
    I am told.

to which my screen hears my reply
    AM I JUST A JAPANESE BEETLE?

If they and I are so alike
    Why am I not allowed to take up space?

But at least I have made my mark on
    The grass.

Rachel Pellom '24

Sol Dhungana '25

Sol Dhungana '25

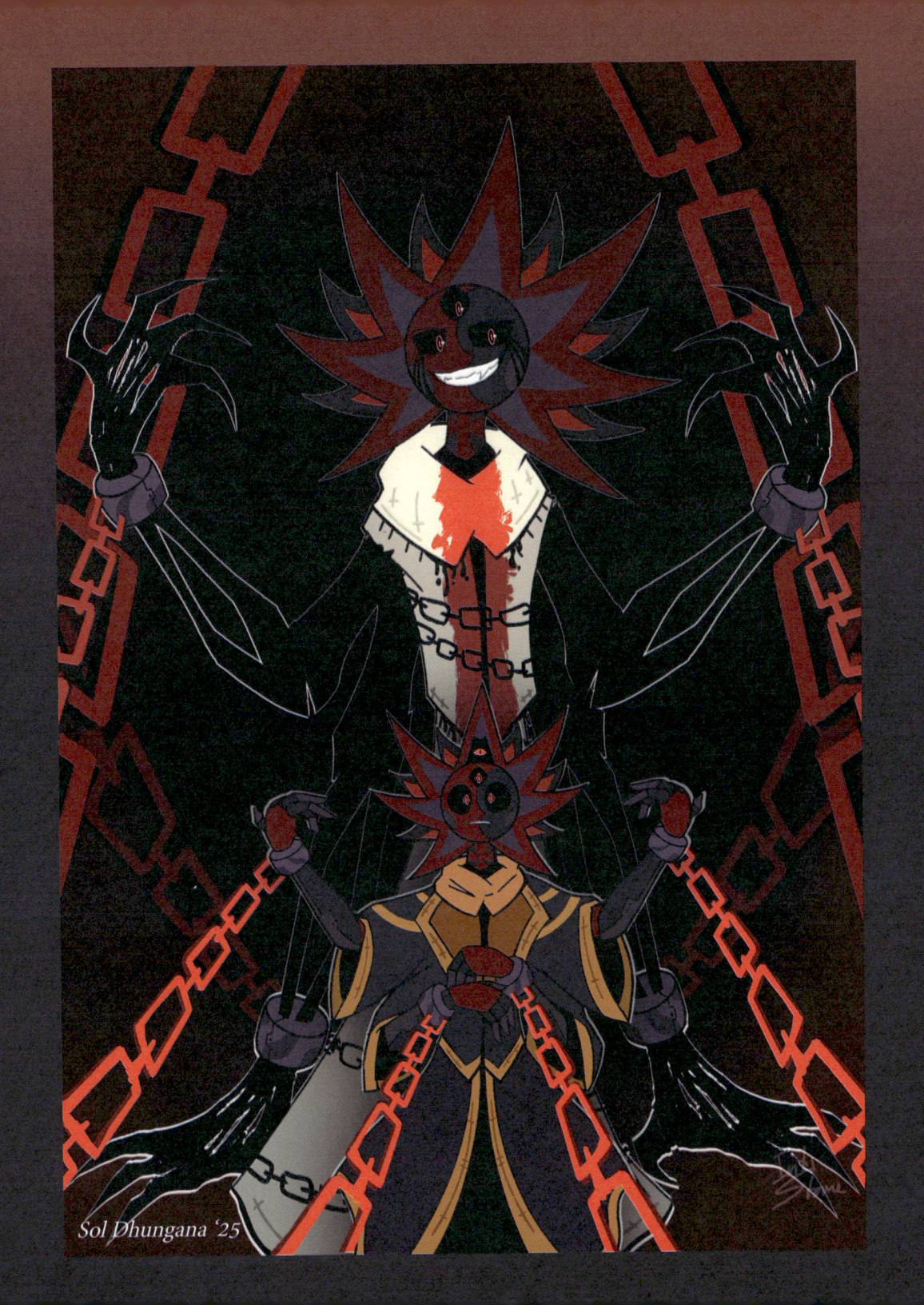

so now ...

Taylor Winstead '24

In my mind
a wave hit me right in my chest,
knocked me down at school
spun me around across states
and spit me back out gasping at a north carolina rest stop

so now I dive into water fully clothed
close my eyes and let waves twist my body to untangle my mind

in my mind
I went weak at the knees and fell before the finish line
people kept running around me and my sisters
we stayed on the ground covered our heads and tried to block out the noise in our homes, heads, and hearts

so now when I run I trip on hope and keep on going

in my mind
It got the kind of somber cold where you can't remember ever feeling anything but cold
chilblains on the hands that used to scratch words on paper, frost on the vocal cords that used to sing, ice on the feet that used to dance

so then when snow fell outside my window
i let cold steal my breath because my voice was coming back,
and I jumped, finally unfrozen, in a midwestern flurry

In my body I was hungry
but my mind sated on empty

so now i feed on life,
drink joy
swallow dreams
tear into life like manna

3rd impact, *Catherine Gao '24*

Mirabelle Smaini '26

Milo King '24

screw you, old man

Jordan Adair, faculty

I was a 10th-grade student living in Lancaster, Pennsylvania, when my father announced one night over dinner that he'd taken a teaching job at William and Mary, and we were moving to Virginia. The news was a complete shock, but it was not the first time my dad had made such declarations. Our family had already moved twice in eight years.

Sitting at the table, I was stunned in silence and seething with anger, ready to explode. My dad argued that it was the right thing for him to do professionally—an argument he had made before—all I could think was that I'm never going to forgive him for taking me away from all the good friends I'd finally found.

You see, my dad has always been a dominating presence in my life, even today. First and foremost, he was a mass of contradictions. The former Marine, the angry disciplinarian, enforcer of rules. At one moment he could be a bully and incredibly mean. At the next, he could be brilliant, caring, and generous. What I feared the most back then was that I'd become more than just his spitting image, so I fought it as hard as I could.

I didn't adjust to my new home very well at all. Those last two years of high school were tough, and my relationship with my Dad sunk to new lows. I started smoking pot and drinking with my new friends and the arguments with my dad grew more frequent, a lot louder, and more intense. By the time I got to college at William and Mary, I did my best to keep my distance to avoid any arguments and visited my Mom whenever he wasn't at home. By this time my parents' marriage was coming to a sad ending after 34 years—what the hell was going on in my life??

The inevitable happened as I neared graduation—one last argument, this time about money. I arrived at our small house on the outskirts of Williamsburg to confront him. I'd always worked while in college, and he'd always paid my tuition, room, and board—until now. I'd overstayed the "four years in college" my father had allotted by a single semester and he wasn't going to pay. I couldn't figure out why—was it out of spite? Was it his usual Jekyl and Hyde personality taking hold? I was furious and so was he and the argument quickly escalated to the usual irrational and loud. But this time was different. Suddenly, he came around the desk, his fists clinched as he yelled, "sometimes you make me so mad I want to hit you!!" I just stood there, not sure what to do, not sure what he was going to do. And then as suddenly as it had started, it was over. I gave in and accepted that he was not going to pay. But that confrontation had scared me—there was that same feeling I'd had as a high school student—was I becoming my father?

I took out a loan to pay for the rest of college, muddled through that last year drinking and smoking dope, graduating near the bottom of my class. I knew I had to get out of town and get away from him, so I planned to move to New England to be near my brother. I was running away, that much I knew, but I had no idea what I was going to do. One of the last things my father said to me before I headed off to Boston after graduation was, "You know, son, I think you'd make a great teacher." All I could think was, "Screw you, old man. What do you know about me anyway?"

I spent the next ten months in Cambridge drifting along, living alone, working as a bartender and waiter, smoking dope, and playing frisbee. I soon realized I had no direction and no purpose, so I thought about what my Dad had said to me when I left—he obviously had seen something of the teacher in me. Or did he just want one of his kids to follow in his footsteps? I wasn't sure, but what did I have to lose—why not try teaching? Not knowing anyone else I might call, I picked up the phone and called my old man for the first time in a *very* long time. It wasn't a long conversation, but I could hear his smug satisfaction coming through loud and clear.

So, I got my certification, trained to teach under some extraordinary mentors, and got my first job teaching in a local public school. That was the start of my career. Soon after that I got married, and in 1988, I finally got clean and sober. No more driving drunk, no more endless parties to nowhere, no more attempts to escape reality. Almost as important, I started counseling to understand my own anger, which was becoming more and more like my dad's. I soon realized that I didn't need to yell and fight with everyone. I may *look* like him, but I didn't have to *be* like him. I could instead be like the good parts of him—the attention to detail, the pride in doing your best work all the time, holding yourself and your students to high standards. That's what I do now in my classes. But to move on, I first had to travel to Williamsburg to make amends so I could own up my half of our difficult relationship.

My wife warned me before I left for Williamsburg: "He's going to get angry when you talk to him. He's going to yell, his voice will get louder with every moment, with every attempt you make at amends. Unless you want it to turn into a screaming match, you are going to have to stay calm, keep your voice even and low and normal. He can't fight if you won't participate." I was nervous for the entire drive to Dad's place, Pam's warning in my head and wondering if I could stand up to him. I arrived at his townhouse, had the usual pleasantries and dinner before we sat down in the living room to chat. He had no real idea why I was there other than for a visit, but the conversation played out just as my wife had predicted. I sat quietly, he yelled, I stayed quiet, he yelled some more, and then finally he settled down. Calm ultimately won out and he accepted my apologies, but it wasn't easy for either of us.

I have always been proud of my father's Marine Corps service during WWII. There's a photograph that hangs on a wall in my classroom today from an event I organized ten years ago in Durham as a part of a Veterans Day ceremony at a local retirement community involving some students of mine and WWII veterans living there. The two of us stand side by side, look-alikes as usual. During the event, my students read tributes to some of the veterans, and I read one I'd written to my Dad. I tried to let him know just how important he was in my life, through all of the good and the bad. And as I read my tribute, I couldn't help but notice that my Dad was crying. Perhaps it was for the pride he had in me or in memory of his time in the Marines. People say I'm the spitting image of my old man, and that picture proves it. But for me, what I see is the peace we finally made with one another as father and son. ♕

her song
Taylor Winstead '24

I hope so many things for you
Things I wish that I'd had too
things I've seen you have to lose
And things I had and wanna watch you choose

I hope your next 10 are better than your last
That you look back with smiles at the past

Remembering your Cat and Jack coat
Instead of how it felt being on a capsized boat

I hope that wicked sense of humor never leaves
that the wicked world stops punishing your youthful naiveté
like Eve's

I want for you to learn the grades you've missed
But if you skip a second of the one you're in I'd be pissed

I want you to have high school without the swish of the
    adolescent ax
Because your elementary days are worse than a john hughes'
    second act

I want for you friends your own age
But that you never hide your old soul, wise and sage

I pray you don't feel like you have to keep being strong
that you get to make bad decisions and be wrong

drink and date and cry and grow and make your parents
    disappointed
But it will be better because your lives won't be so disjointed

I pray that voice in your head, you run it off
And when someone older condescends you roll your eyes
and scoff

One day you will look at a dorm and miss your dad,
And the next day have a fight on the phone and get mad

Then call him up and say you want to see him
because it's your choice, no longer made by them

And one day you will be the same person through and
through
But each piece of your life will be picked by you, and it will
be tried and true.

Mai Malesky '25

melt together
Blake Roper '24

All the frozen treats dread May
On the hottest, summer, sunny day
Though their love was sweetly bizarre
The ice cream loved the candy bar.

The summer smelt of sweetened sorrow
The lovers would melt by early 'morrow
Ice cream said, "You are my star.
I'll never love another, candy bar."

Their love, the sun never did condone
Yet ice cream smiled atop her cone
But the peaceful pain was scarcely felt
They laughed once more as they slowly melt.

The puddle of lovers felt quite ill
But they said 'I love you' still
Candy Bar said happily then,
"For you darling I'd melt all over again!"

Catherine Gao '24

injuries of time

Madeline Gottfried '24

    Nothing can ever be as whimsical as the pure freedom of girlhood, blissfully separate from the horrors of a world where I must learn how to merge on the highway. The magic of my youth was preserved by the protection of those around her who sought to keep me from the thorns on the rose vine or to catch me when the Newfoundland pushed me down the front steps of our house. Magic was alive in the heart of this girl as she insisted on whispering a wish into a penny and tossing it into a fountain whenever she had the chance. Alive when I would spin in circles to wash the sadness away, getting so dizzy that I didn't know what had hurt me so badly in the first place. Alive as I read the stories of Annie and Jack or Ivy and Bean, wishing that I too could make a volcano out of the pile of dirt in my front lawn. Alive when I stuck my head out the car window and watched the trees fly past me.

But seventeen is a rotten age. And it hurt. It hurts. Because in the end there is no protection; the magic of the world will slowly crumble away before your eyes. The whimsy I knew before has crumbled away. I fell out of the tree and broke my arm. I grew out of my favorite pink frilly dress. I walked barefoot on the concrete streets of my neighborhood after a fight with my mom. I dented my forehead on a bookshelf at Pier 1. I sobbed when I found the Christmas elf in the drawer of my mother's dresser. I changed, I drifted, I lost my sliver of normalcy, I let go of what I love, I'll find myself endlessly overflowing with tears.

In the end, as much as you can try to take the girl away from the magic, you can't take the magic out of the girl. The heartbreak of my youth doesn't have to limit my future. I make a wish whenever I spot 11:11 on the clock; I can rejuvenate the whimsy of my youth as I live away from the protection that crumbled away during my childhood. Now, I spill my deepest secrets to my mother. I fill my iPhone's notes app with poetry and anecdotes. I feel the winter chill turn my nose bright red. I set myself free into the forest of my backyard and sing my heart out to the songs of Alex G and Big Thief. If all else fails and I find myself completely alone with my oh so tragic feelings, I can cry my eyes out to Elliott Smith and The Velvet Underground until the pain washes away. When it's the start of fall and the weather is perfectly crisp I can sit in the hammock and listen to Foxygen and Cub. I have learned that there is truly nothing that a no name song or retro girl band can't fix. No matter what I do, it'll change. I'll change. I'll leave girlhood behind me.

Catherine Gao '24

woman of fewer words

Blake Roper '24

Father says I talk too much
Babbles that I'm out of touch

And now my quick mouth must repose
For now I speak in lines of prose

So much to say with such little time
Since I must talk with rhythm and rhyme

My yammering forced to be concise
And every word must be precise

And now with every stanza's end
Beyond the lines you must pretend

Even though my prose is done
My story's only just begun.

Sol Dunghana '25

monetizing happiness

Taylor Winstead '24

The sounds of ringing echoed around the large bank hall. Tellers somewhat cheerfully exchanged happiness chips, self-love coins, and emotional regulation bits. David, currently in the process of transferring a staggering amount of happiness chips from the account of one Jasmine Dunlap to someone called Daren James, wondered why emotional regulation bits were seeing such a spurt in popularity. Most likely the coming of the holidays. An election year, the prospect of family meals, and Christmas shopping, had people desperate to pick up some extra shifts at work so some extra tokens could go towards their ability to emotionally regulate whatever shit their family had going on.

"Ma'am, you're going to need to step forward please so that we can upload this transfer." David hated this part of his job, especially when it had to do with happiness coins. He tapped the button on his screen that said, "Transaction completed. Ready to upload." He lifted the scanner to Jasmine Dunlap's forehead. She looked young. The scanner beeped as it adjusted her serotonin levels to reflect her balance. The effect was immediate. A light in her eyes dimmed. Her smile became forced, and painful. Poor girl. Hopefully she'd get a windfall soon.

He looked down in the midst of issuing her an empty "good day," and saw something stuck in between the slats of his desk, something copper. As she walked away, he pulled it out, and was shocked to find that it was an old fashioned quarter, from the days of the gold standard. He pocketed it, wishing for one brief moment with all his heart that things could go back to the old ways.

As Jasmine Dunlap walked away, she fought that sluggish, weighted-down feeling that always came with a rush of depression. Already susceptible to unhelpful and circular thoughts now because of her abysmal bank account, she felt herself fixate on the series of unfortunate decisions she had made leading up to this moment. Allowing Liam from the office to convince her to get a drink. Which led to her getting wasted because she'd been stupid and gave away some positive coping skill pieces that day to her friend Sarah, who, yes, desperately needed them, but by drink number four she was feeling the loss. Then allowing herself to get roped into that stupid bet — that she could land all five darts on the dart board when she knew she had terrible aim. And then, worst of all, allowing herself to bet 5000 happiness chips on it. 5,000 happiness chips was 200 work tokens. That was more than 3 months' wages ... She was so stupid ... so stupid ... so stupid ... the thought became obsessive. That's what happens, she told herself, when you start off with unnaturally low serotonin levels anyway, and then you blow your happiness chips on impressing some dumb guy. You end up severely depressed.

Taylor Winstead '24

She knew she had to visit her sibling after this, and they, the older of the two, would not be happy about any of this. She groaned as she imagined facing work the next day. On her drive home she saw a rusty billboard advertising for talk therapy — First Session Free!! She chuckled grimly to herself, "Good luck with that." When the very chemicals and hormones of everyones' bodies were externally manipulated, there is only so much that talk therapy can do. What a dying industry — she felt bad for anyone who got their degree expecting to help people, and now found themselves in this nightmare.

Her phone rang. She picked up. It was her sibling, Joy Dunlap.

"Sis, what did you do?!" they screeched. "I saw your account!"

"You need to stop figuring out all of my passwords to things and then snooping around," Jasmine shot back.

They bickered, as siblings do, with Jasmine putting forth as much energy as she could, but of course, still feeling drained and fatigued.

When they hung up Joy Dunlap sighed, spinning in their chair behind their desk at the university. If they were being honest with themselves, they had only called their sister as an excuse to procrastinate their dissertation —
 "Monetizing Happiness: With Late Stage Capitalism, Money Can Buy Everything." ♛

Rachel Pellom '24

the lost canto

Ananya Mettu '26, Audrey Crowder '26,
Fiona Lawton '26, & Joanna Yoon '26

Upon our descent from the giant's fetid palm
The veil of uncertainty descended on my weary complexion.
As the bride on her wedding day puts salt in her pocket

And avoids the gentle gaze of her soon-to-be spouse
While the bridesmaid assuages her trepidation,
So does my mentor as he strikes a blow across my apprehensive brow.

"Son, do not now falter in your liturgical journey.
He does not welcome unsteadiness of faith
And she who waits will turn away from your vacillating visage."

And I: "As always, you steer me away
From my qualms, regardless of how ponderous they may be."
And my sagacious guide continued on our bless'd course with a nod.

The shrill lament of unrighteous guardians pierced my ears
As I beheld the sight: pungent liquid of a reddish hue soaked the land
Bloodlike tears seeping into the very crevices of the dolorous air itself.

"O learned one, what is that which falls from above?"
And he: "It is that which flows in the veins of the young babes who are so ill-treated by the ones who were meant to shield them from such harm."

As I traversed the slippery terrain of crimson,
I came across a shade much too familiar to the eye.
"Please, man. It's Dan Schneider here, help me out…"

"…all I did was try to make some kids famous."
While the words entered my encephalon with ease,
It did not align with my Florentine cognition.

"Master, what is this foreign tongue in which he speaks?"
To this, my wise one replied, "It is the way of the future
To speak in this broken verse."

The tattooed shade laments, "I just wanted to be close with them;
We were just homies, you know?"
This rapacious shade had used his charges like puppets on a jagged string.

For this pungent sin it is only fit
That the demons keep a watchful eye
The piercing glare of the black orb never seemed to stray from the sinners' every move.

"What is this vile creature that appears to be a juncture between machinery and flesh?"
To this the, shade replied,
"Bro, you don't know what a camera is? Boomer."

I was growing weary of this pathetic, diminutive shade of a man,
And my master, seeming to sense my distress,
Led me away from this blood-soaken ditch.

Sol Dhungana '25

Rachel Pellom '24

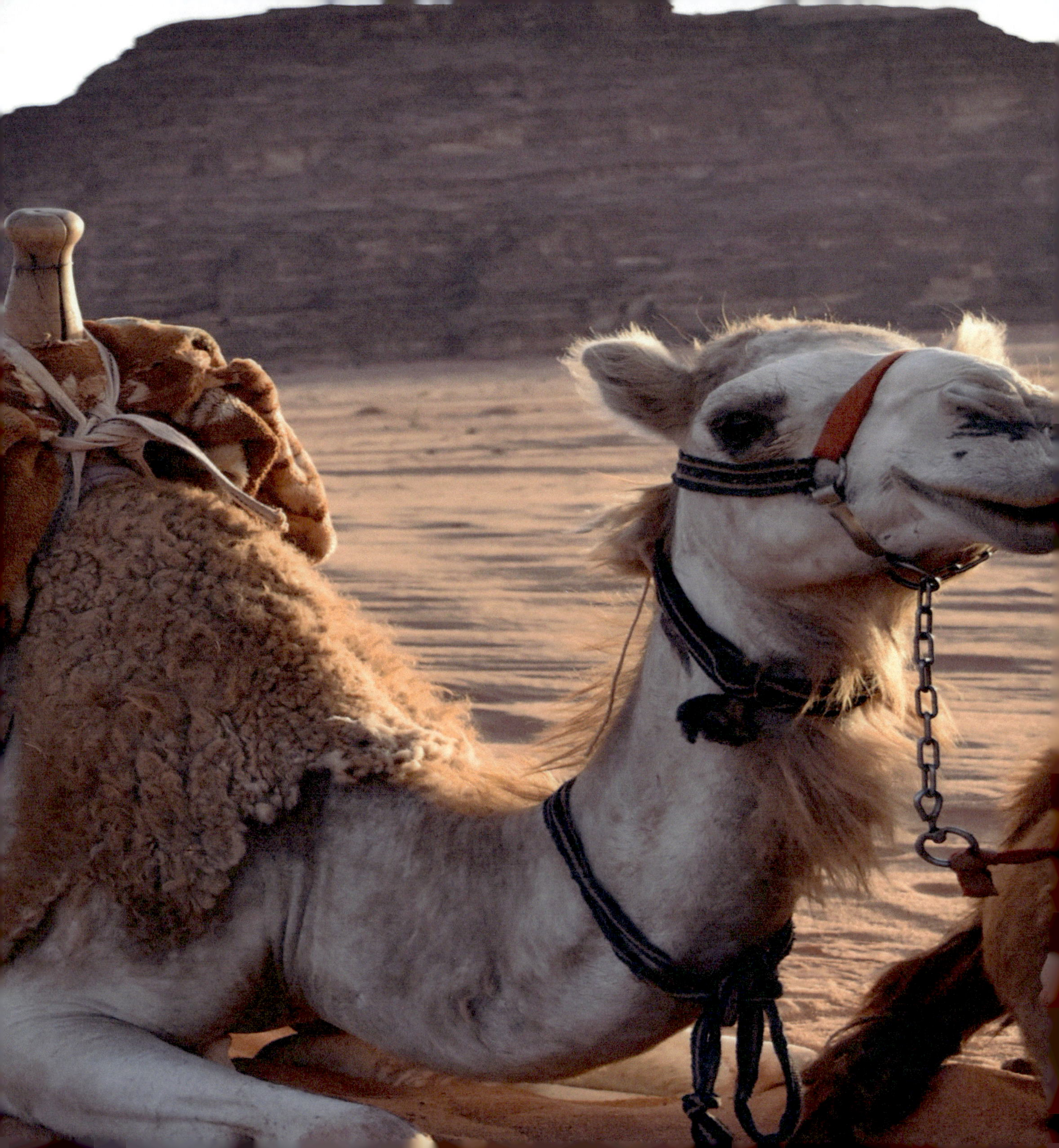

arodnap mansion
Taylor Winstead '24

> Perhaps you are looking for a more idyllic life for your children. Maybe you need to upsize a little bit. Perhaps you're just intrigued. In any case, Arodnap Manor, a palatial estate in the mountains of Vermont, is available for purchase! Arodnap is a historical goldmine of information and relics. Built in the late 1800's by an esteemed scholar of the classics, it is home to some of the most treasured artifacts and archeological finds of classical antiquity. The home has been refurbished to include all trappings of modern comfort, and includes an indoor pool! Enjoy the many acres of grounds surrounding Arodnap that include gardens, walking and hiking trails, and several small lakes.
>
> The only requirement is 500 dollars and a promise: for three days (from Oct 29th-31st) each year, you will close all of the windows, lock all of the doors, and STAY INSIDE.
>
> Thanks for your interest: to learn more see the QR code!

The sheaf of paper was poking out from her mother's purse, where it sat on the floor of the car in front of Jamie. Jamie rolled her eyes and went back to the book on Greek myth that she was reading.

Her parents were stupid people. Lots of kids think they know better than their parents, and rarely is it true. This time it was true. Her parents were the kind of people who "borrowed" some of her money to get a tattoo of each other's names on their shoulders while drunk that they would later regret when they were fighting or not speaking. They were both reasonably well-off. Trust fund kids who'd blown through most of it in college, but still had enough left over to make dumb decisions. But this had to be the stupidest of all decisions that they had ever made. It practically screamed either a practical joke, or the sick beginning of a horror movie. She'd looked up the guy that used to own it. He was the kind of creepy that leans towards campy. He led insane experiments, believed he could "resurrect the classics," whatever that meant, etc … so on and so forth. It was cool — what 9 year old girl in her Wednesday Addams emo Avril Lavigne fuck the system phase doesn't love camp? Okay, so maybe nine is a little bit of an odd age to have that phase, but Jamie had always been an overachiever.

When they got to Arodnap, it was October 28th, and her parents immediately launched into a full scale exploration of all the things in the house they could sell for cash. The cool grotesque statues and gargoyles. Everything absurd, and whimsical, and creepy. It was all a cash grab. This could have been a story about a preteen girl living in a haunted house, although lord knows we've got enough of those.

Evan Fields '24

But her parents stopped that from being a possibility. They seemed unconcerned, and excited. She holed up in her room reading her Greek myths book and wondered if they were all going to die come tomorrow, or if it was going to be revealed that they were on some insane prank show. There was a part of her that wanted something horrible to happen, self-destructive as it was, so that she could be right. The day before they left she had thrown an old-school temper tantrum arguing that no, they shouldn't trust a random flier found on the side of the street, nor should they trust the half a dozen emails exchanged back and forth between a shadowy real estate agent. No one had cared.

That night she went behind her parents and double checked that they had locked every door and every window tight. They had forgotten several side doors — it was a big house after all — and a flash of fear ran through her. It was a fear that she normally suppressed, but one that crept through in these moments nevertheless — that she was completely responsible for her life. No one was there to fix it, or hold her pain, or keep her safe. Next to one of the doors, ARODNAP was carved, etched, into the wall. What a weird name. Normally it would be cool. Now it just made her mad. She kicked the wall and went to bed.

When she woke the next morning and felt nothing bad happening, she breathed out shakily. Downstairs her dad was making pancakes, a rare sign of foresight and planning. Even more shockingly, a rare sign of caring for others. She chewed the blueberry dough suspiciously, looking around. Her heart clenched as she realized that she would have to follow her parents around for the next three days making sure they didn't open any of the doors. They were the type of people that thought rules applied to everyone but them.

At first it was fine. She kept them within eyeshot for about two and a half days. Helping them with chores, suggesting they play board games, reading with one eye always looking towards their location. It was, ironically, the 31st, when everything fell apart.

She went to the bathroom for five minutes. She was timing it. That's how paranoid she was. Arodnap was etched in the wall of the bathroom again. As she looked up from the sink she caught sight of the etching in the mirror. PANDORA.

Shit.

Right at that moment, she heard a door creaking open. She came running out of the bathroom, a sudden knowledge clanging in her brain. Her mom was holding it open when they heard a scuffling, and in scuttled what was clearly Anger, with Lust not far behind.

Well … Jamie thought … no telling what was gonna happen next. At least now she understood what he meant by "resurrect the classics."

Catherine Gao '24

how i pass the time in despair

Lilly Zellman '24

It's been said a thousand times: music should make the listener feel something. Beethoven makes me feel like a wealthy and immoral aristocrat who kicks stray kittens. Nirvana makes me feel like I haven't taken a shower in a couple days. Taylor Swift makes me feel like saying, "Screw you, I'm in my Reputation era" whenever someone offers me the slightest bit of criticism, which inevitably leaves me with a few burned bridges and a lot of regrets. Once I've fought the felines, passed out from my own smell, and lost all my friends, I need a different type of music. I crave the kind of music that will make up for the damage done by classical, rock, and bubble-gum pop. Classical music's wordless string quartet can't convince me that everything will work out in the end. Similarly, Nirvana's odes of teen spirit and fiery lakes don't exactly scream words of encouragement. Excruciatingly so, no matter how many songs Taylor Swift writes about the drop-dead-gorgeous boy-next-door, I will never find missed romantic connections and slow burns to be in sync with the inner turmoil I am facing. Instead, I find solace in the tales of dead friends, impending doom, and starless skies offered by Phoebe Bridgers.

Oftentimes I find myself regretting the bond I formed with her music; however, I am tied to Phoebe Bridgers the way Jacob Black imprinted himself upon Renesmee Cullen in Twilight (minus the whole ushy-gushy-romantic, slightly pedophilic part). Phoebe Bridgers's music is so depressing that listening to her songs makes me wallow around in sadness and despair. So naturally I ask myself, what makes Phoebe Bridgers's music so good? If these songs make me feel like I want to spin around in a microwave and then be tossed into the bottom of the ocean, why do I keep listening? My obvious conclusion, with Phoebe herself as my guide, is her words. Phoebe's lyrics aren't as simple as, "I, I, I shake it off, I shake it off!" Instead, lines like "The sirens go all night/I used to joke that if they woke you up/Somebody better be dying" from Phoebe's song "Halloween" feel like a warm, razor-edged embrace. When consumed in the form of a two chapter reading assignment, words can feel like the enemy, but Phoebe Bridgers's lyrics feel like the words of an old friend who can't fully support your actions in the present because they remember the innocent you of 2019, but loved you then and, for that reason, love you now. Phoebe Bridgers uses metaphors, hyperboles, similes, and all the other painful parts of a 5th grade figurative language lesson in English class to bring these complicated feelings to life, which is my answer to the question, "How does Phoebe Bridgers use rhetorical devices in her lyrics to enhance her songs?"

Phoebe Bridgers claims that she uses figurative language to "make a song better." Hearing that there is truly no rhyme or reason to her lyrical madness is defeating, but these same words that are used to "make a song better" are described by critics as "grotesque and unsparing;" "intimate, fragile, real;" and the product of a "lacerating wit." So, I figure that if Phoebe claims her lyrics are really nothing more than equivalent to a free hour spent on Garageband and the news deems her as a lyrical genius, there has got to be a spot in the middle. My process follows along the lines of 80% self-indulgence and 20% actual scientific work by listening to every song that Phoebe Bridgers has written and selecting a couple lines where I could clearly see use of figurative language.

In her 2017 debut album *Stranger in the Alps*, themes of loss and connection make up 11 songs that must have been hard to digest in the same year that Ed Sheeran dropped "Shape of You." Track #2 "Motion Sickness" puts the listener in the shoes of Phoebe Bridgers's ex-boyfriend Ryan Adams who, frighteningly so, was in a band when Phoebe was born and subsequently gave her emotional motion sickness. One of the most important lyrics from the song is, "There are no words in the English language/I could scream to drown you out." Now, according to the beloved dictionary dot com, the average 20 year old knows 40,000 words of the English language. Maybe Phoebe is unfamiliar with the dictionary, but I am willing to bet that at least 39,000 of these words could be screamed so loud that the boyfriends of old would sink straight to the bottom of the dead sea. However, I don't think Phoebe Bridgers would date someone who couldn't swim, and unless she's lost her voice, there are a variety of words she can scream making this an excellent hyperbole. This line has gotten the song 259 plus million plays on Spotify alone, and it evokes feelings of resentment and empathy from its listeners. Another notable piece of figurative language on this album comes from "Smoke Signals" where Phoebe sings, "We'll watch TV while the lights on the street/Put all the stars to death." If I was to go outside instead of staying in my room 24/7 listening to Phoebe's music, I would definitely see some stars; however, I don't do that so this will remain an excellent hyperbole.

Not to exaggerate, but *Punisher* is one of the best albums on planet Earth. This extraterrestrial, moody, Grammy- nominated album is the best display of Phoebe Bridgers's influences: Fleetwood Mac, Elliot Smith, and Nirvana, all known for their extremely fleshed out lyrics. This album is the definition of loving someone and wanting to kill them because of that. The feeling is extremely present in the songs "ICU" and "Moon Song," which are coincidentally my favorite two songs off the album. In "ICU," the lyrics start off with a series of things that the narrator hates about the person she loves, but after a while she says, "I feel something when I see you now." One of the most important digs that Phoebe takes at this other person, who she actually revealed to be Marshall Vore, her drummer, is, "If you're a work of art/I'm standing too close/I can see the brush strokes." Ouch. The reverse personification of someone as a painting along with the juxtaposition of a work of art and some hasty brushwork creates a beautifully complex dynamic between the singer and her muse.

The pain doesn't end there. "Moon Song," is an ode to all the people who take "Find Your Love Language" quizzes and are almost disappointed to find out that they might be "acts of service" people. Just because it might be true doesn't mean it wouldn't be exhausting, which is why the line, "So I will wait for the next time you want me/Like a dog with a bird at your door" hurts the way it does. Creating this simile of Phoebe as a dog waiting to surprise its owner with a dead bird emotionally sucks, because what kind of person is going to look at a bloody dead bird and say, "Wow! All this for me?" This R-rated Marley & Me stings but also vividly explains Phoebe's feelings for whoever's door it is she sings about. The simile lends itself to a bird motif present in the rest of the song, "When you saw the dead little bird you started crying, but you know the killer doesn't understand" exploring the continuous power of a single simile in a song.

Margaret Jester '24

Along with releasing both *Stranger in the Alps* and *Punisher*, Phoebe Bridgers can be heard in the songs of other artists like Bright Eyes, Better Oblivion Community Center, Taylor Swift, and the Minions Soundtrack. This diverse discography presents fans with a continuous timeline of Phoebe's music, especially considering she delivers excellent lyrics when in a band. This year, the supergroup boygenius, composed of best friends Julien Baker, Lucy Dacus, and Phoebe Bridgers, rocked the world with their first album titled *the record*, a welcome album after the group's five year absence. Earning them the title of the new Nirvana, boygenius's *the record* changed absolutely everything for the fans of each of these artists and, most of all, me in my bedroom. The way boygenius operates is that half of the songs on the album are written completely by an individual member and the other songs contain verses written by each member, rather than the whole song. "Cool About It" by boygenius is an example of verses written by each musician. The group setting only enhances Phoebe's literary divinity. Phoebe sings, "Once I took your medication to know what it's like/And now I have to act like I can't read your mind." Even though I try very hard to read minds so that I can avoid any semblance of the unknown, I know that it is impossible to do so, which is why this hyperbole strikes such a chord with myself and many other listeners — it's a little gross to think about taking drugs that don't belong to me and reading minds would put me in an eternal state of whiplash.

Phoebe's use of figurative language in her music is nauseating. It's gross, it's sickening, it's absolutely off the wall bonkers. And yet, the fact that her lyrics can make listeners feel these emotions is amazing. Phoebe Bridgers's lyrics are a sign that maybe I should pay attention in English class during DIDOFS analyses. So long are the days of evil Beethoven aristocracy and bad blood with Taylor Swift. Using figurative language to make her music better, Phoebe Bridgers's music makes me feel like I'm in a tight friendship with the moon, like I can decipher good lyrics from bad lyrics, and like I have objectively superior music taste.

Rachel Pellom '24

Olivia Rivers '24

135

mountain story continued...

The orange glow of the rising sun spurred them all into action: it was day two and they needed to start early if they were going to make it on time up the steepest section of the trail yet. Astrid and Leo had woken first, packing up the cooking supplies and waking up the others. Daphne had bargained for ten more minutes. Margot was put in charge of packing up the tent she had slept in that night and Daphne was in charge of the other. Astrid was charting their path for the day, while Leo and Max organized the food and supplies into everyone's packs.

Around thirty minutes later, the packs were stuffed full, the trail ahead laid out, and one tent put away. But the other remained standing.

"Daphne," Astrid called out, coldly. Daphne turned around from where she stood next to the tent, toothbrush in her mouth, a confused look on her face.

"What?" Daphne sputtered out. Astrid's face twisted.

"I just don't understand how you don't realize that you being slow to wake up and slow to help inconveniences all of us," Astrid's cheeks flamed red. "Like, do you not see that we're all packed up? Do you not realize that this was your idea in the first place? We're not going to fucking make it if you can't handle getting your ass up and going. We're all doing our part to make your goddamn idea become a reality." Astrid stormed over and started deconstructing the tent, pulling apart pieces and shoving them into the tent-bag one after the other until it was completely down. Daphne could only stand and watch. Her chin was quivering but she didn't cry.

"You know not everyone is fucking perfect like you! Not everything can go the exact way you want it. We're gonna make it either way, learn to take a fucking break once and a while," Daphne retorted losing her battle against the tears.

"Maybe if you were better at following instructions, I would be able to take a break!"

"You're not my mother, Astrid, stop acting like it!" And with that Astrid went silent. Only the chirping of the birds could be heard as Daphne snatched the tent bag from Astrid's frozen hands and stuffed it into her pack. Silent still, Astrid hoisted her own pack back onto her back and walked toward the trail.

Margot watched Daphne whisper to Leo, hands wiping tears, mouth turned pointedly downwards. It was not uncommon for Astrid to blow up because of disorganization, but it had never been this big before. Around thirty minutes into the hike Daphne seemed to have gotten over the verbal abuse thrown at her, and found herself in a harmless quarrel with Leo. Margot was glad she was okay, Daphne never let things haunt her. But Astrid's prolonged silence irked Margot in a way she couldn't ignore. One thing Astrid wasn't was quiet.

Filled with the energy of instant coffee, soggy oatmeal, and the prettiest weather they'd had thus far, Margot found herself speeding to the front of the group as they hiked into the afternoon hours. As she had been since the beginning of the trip, Astrid was leading the group, her calculated steps navigating the rough terrain for the rest of them to follow. She was fast, but Margot was determined to match her pace. While Leo argued with Daphne in the middle of the group and Max mediated from his spot in the back, Astrid had been focusing all her attention on ensuring the safety and timeliness of the crew of eighteen-year-olds.

"How are you, Astrid?" Margot asked, a bit more out of breath than she'd like to admit, finally reaching her pace.

"I'm good," Astrid smiled with her eyes. Smiles with eyes, Margot had found, are much different than smiles

"I'm good," Astrid smiled with her eyes. Smiles with eyes, Margot had found, are much different than smiles with wide mouths and wrinkled noses. Smiles with eyes don't mean a thing.

"To be honest, Astrid, I really don't think you are," Margot offered, tentatively. "I mean that blow up at Daphne this morning …" She trailed off, knowing she was teetering on thin ice. But Astrid didn't furrow her brows, grimace or deny. Instead, she turned her head abruptly away from Margot's view, staring aggressively out at the mountain ranges before them. Her breathing was deep and forced. Margot saw the tremble of her chin before Astrid could take a big breath, swallow her distress, and turn back to her, the slightest red having appeared in her eyes.

"I'm …," she began, and after a moment, finally blurted out, "this whole trip has honestly been so hard. It's like, I can't put it into words but I feel really out of control. I'm so scared about Leo, and Daph is always doing something insane, and Max is obviously not doing okay mentally and for some reason I cannot get away from the feeling that it is all my fault, my responsibility."

"Oh, Astrid, I promise you it's not. Everyone is responsible for themselves, it's not your fault at all," Margot comforted, noticing the tears in her eyes well up once again, then disappearing as Astrid forced them away with another deep breath.

"I know, my mom tells me that too. But I can't escape this urge to make everything go my way. It feels like without following my plan, everything will go to shit. Everything is going to shit right now. Daph was right, I act too much like a parent." Astrid's fists were clenching beside her as she continued, "And listen, Marg, you're doing great and I know they can handle themselves. But, I feel so sick everytime I think about the fact that after this summer, when we come down from this mountain, I won't be there to make sure they're okay, to give them a last-minute ride, to make sure they eat. I can't heal whatever Leo has, I can't tell Daph that the guy she's talking to is a dick, I can't help you ace that test, and I can't save Max from his own mind. Once we leave, it's up to them. I love them, I love you. Everything is too uncertain."

Her control was her love in action. She wanted everything to go smoothly because the fear of her friends' unhappiness paralyzed her. Margot understood. She squeezed Astrid's hand in understanding and allowed her to change the subject. They focused on their feet as they talked: the terrain was rocky and sharp, one misstep and a broken shin could be your fate. Eventually the two fell silent as their huffs of exertion overcame their conversation. By noon, the group was exhausted and dripping with sweat

They took their lunch of pb&j's underneath the shade of a large tree around three quarters of the way up their ascent. Hands shakily spread the peanut butter on the bread, mouths scarfed down the much needed fuel. Margot's eyes watched Astrid make her way over to the root Daphne was sitting on.

"I was not fair. You don't deserve the things I said. I promise my anger wasn't for you, it's been there for a while," Astrid admitted sitting beside Daphne.

"I know. I'm sorry I am not keeping us on track. I get caught up in time. You are one of my best friends, Astrid, I accept your apology and I know you don't say things out of hate," Daphne smiled, offering her a sip of her water.

"I'm okay, thanks. I just … please don't be afraid to call out my bullshit. I can be an asshole sometimes," she chuckled. Daphne hugged her.

"You're my favorite asshole, Astrid."

After lunch a new found energy ran through the group. One fourth of the ascent left and they hiked it quicker than any other section. Of course, at times the group found themselves using both their feet and hands to propel themselves up the slope, but their bear-like crawls managed to help them make good time. The rest of the day's hike was a flatter one. Trees shaded the trail casting flitting shadows over their path. The air was less humid and the group's sweat evaporated quickly, cooling them down. Although, Margot found her breaths harder to take, as if two breaths only counted for one. Nevertheless, she was overwhelmed with joy when the campsite they settled on was a perfectly flat clearing. She knew the stargazing would be unforgettable.

"Hey, come check out this spot," Daphne grabbed her arm as the sun made its way below the skyline that night. The camp was set up, Astrid was comforting a still sick Leo by the fire, and Max was boiling water for his noodles.

Daphne pulled Margot down a small path adjacent to the campsite and they pushed through tall shrubbery until they came out onto a rock ledge. A breeze ran over Margots cheeks and nose as she stood in awe once again of the sight before her. Blue-lit mountains and valleys, the stars mingling with the leftover light of the now set sun.

"Daph, oh my goodness, you found a gem. This is insane."

"I know right?" Daphne asked, ecstatic. "Sit with me." And so Margot did. The two girls talked and talked about memories as far back as freshman year track and field and as recent as a final paper in a dreaded senior year English class. Slowly, as the stars grew brighter, they fell into a lull of peaceful silence.

Daphne's face was flushed under her eyes, her gaze shifting slowly from the stars to the skyline of mountains and back to the stars. Margot watched her go back and forth, her hand tracing the craters in the rock of the lookout.

"What is it about him?" Margot asked, gaze falling into Daphne's same pattern. Daphne didn't look at her but her mouth pulled tight into a grimace.

"Sometimes it feels like I am just waiting for them to screw up," she sighed. She sniffled.

"Ha, I feel that. But there's more…"

"It is so painful. When a guy finally says something that reminds you that you are only part human to him. It happens everytime, and yet I still hold out hope that someone will invest in my whole soul and not just my body, what I give, how I make them look."

"So this new guy…"

"Do you want to know what he fucking said?" she scoffed. "We were talking about how we haven't seen each other for a while. I reminded him that just a few days ago we had gone on a study date. It was really cute, lattes and snack breaks and …" she trailed off, choking on the pain in the back of her throat Margot knew was there. "He said that it didn't count."

"Wait, what?" Margot asked, turning to her.

"We didn't hook up, Marg. That was the one date he didn't get to fuck me," she was crying now. "That's why it didn't count." She laughed through her tears, that sad, giving up kind of laugh.

"God, Daph," they locked eyes, and just sat there together understanding, heads on each other's shoulders. After a while, Daphne lifted her head.

"I'm sick of pretending it's not breaking me. No guy ever wanting to actually know me. Always listening and never listened too. I just want to be a girl. I don't want to be a number on some dick's scale based on how big my tits are and how submissive I act. I want to workout without being stared at. I want to have my girly things and not get shit for it. I want my value to be based on how loving I am, how creative I am, and how ambitious I am. Fuck, Margot, I've written a novel at 18. But it's 'what's your body count?'"

She was gasping in between sentences. Her tears streamed, heavy, down her cheeks. Margot watched them fall.

"I'm scared, Daphne," Margot admitted, her own teary eyes meeting hers. "I'm scared because I can't make it go away or tell you it's going to get better. I watch the way my dad treats my mom. He had the nerve to watch golf while she set up my entire graduation party. Hell, she raised me, not him. I'm sick of it, too. I'm sick of being told I'm the instigator of the family because I call out the men in my family for their misogyny. I'm sick of feeling shame for our pain."

Daphne held her hand and she squeezed it back. In that moment, she let the fear and sickness and exhaustion leave her and she felt safe. It is a difficult thing to be a teenage girl. People hear you, but no one really listens. Margot was not some teenage boy's sick fantasy: compliant, sexy, unquestioning. Margot was a gentle, artistic, hurt, angry, strong, and complex person. She thought, right there on the rock overlooking the mountains and the stars, how she would not give up being a girl for anything. Daphne sat beside her thinking the same.

Soon, Astrid called their names in distress and they went running back to the campsite. Margot and Daphne went right to hug her. A commiserating kind of hug but a prideful one too: they were lucky enough to have each other as sisters in this world that sometimes felt so cruel.

Quickly, the group's focus turned to setting up camp. It was dark and they all began arguing about who had what tent back and who was cleaning up what.

"All I'm saying is if we don't cowboy camp here, when the hell else are we going to?" Daphne exclaimed to Leo as they organized the food. Margot's interest was piqued.

"What's cowboy camping?" She asked.

"The best way to camp, Marg. No tent. Just you, your sleeping bag, and the stars," Daphne's eyes had their signature twinkle. Margot's heart fluttered.

"I cannot explain to you how badly I want to do that," Margot said.

"Yes, we have to, it's perfect. Please Leo, convince Astrid for me?"

"Fine. It would be so sick, I can't deny that," Leo agreed, and set off to persuade Astrid to agree to the idea.

Daphne got her wish. After a luxurious, and very late dinner of pot noodles, only the sleeping bags and a tarp were removed from their packs. The sleeping bags were lined in a row upon the tarp and the group settled in for bed.

It was serene: laying beside all of your friends, staring up at the infinite sky, no phones, no deadlines, no pressures. It was existence at its purest for Margot. She gazed around the scene. The milky way shone bright in the purple soup of the sky, stars twinkled unhindered by light pollution, satellites sped through the scene, the moon watched over it all. It was beautiful, but her friends outshone it by far. Peaceful faces all watching the sky, comfortable silence, cheeks aglow with moonlight: charming. She was charmed.

Evan Fields '24

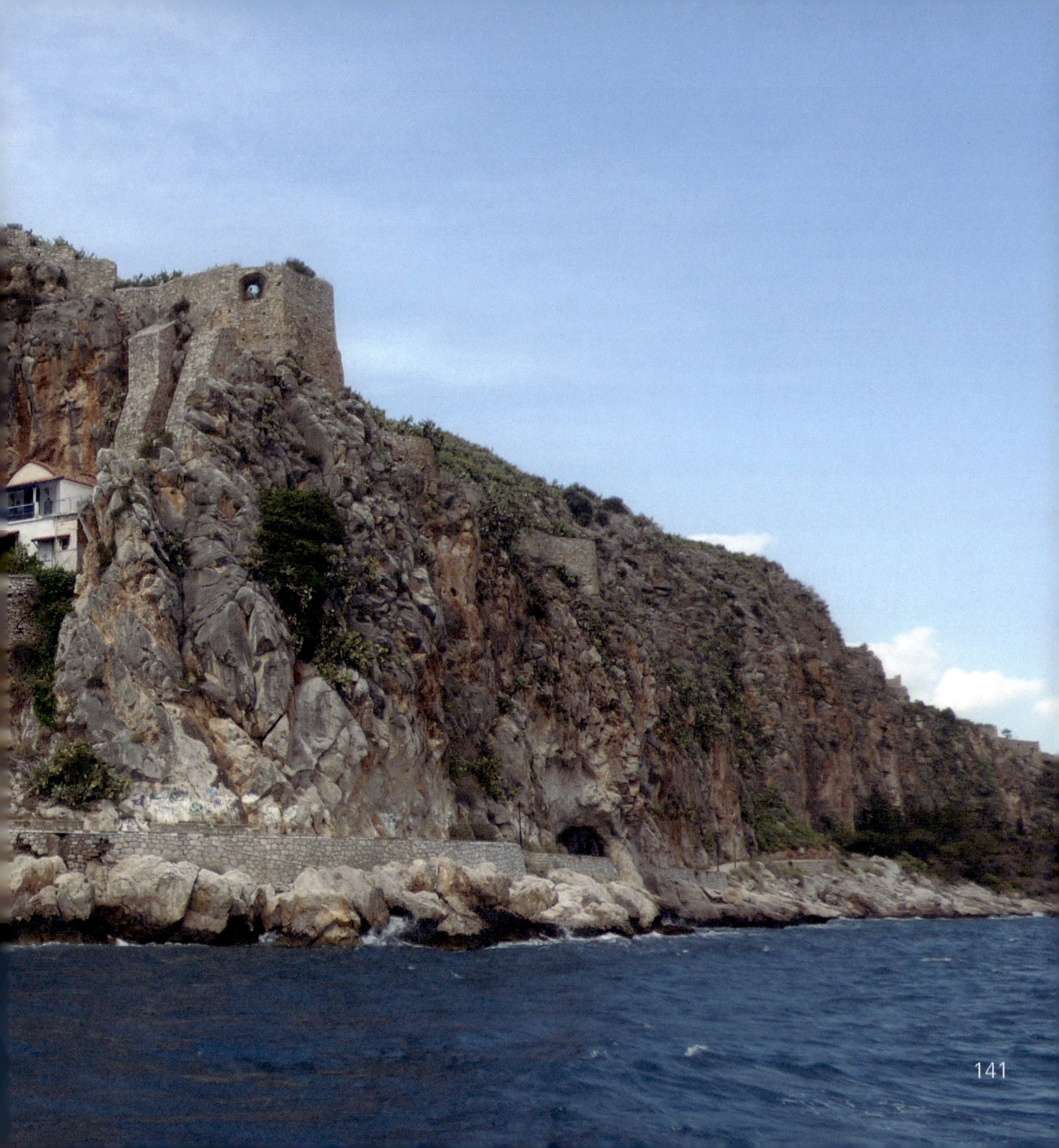

Margot forgot about how charmed she was the second she woke up damp as mists of light rain fell over the group.

"Oh so fuck us then?" Max groaned, getting out of his wet sleeping bag and wiping the rain out of his eyes.

"Shit guys, I'm so sorry I didn't know it was gonna rain," Daphne said nervously.

"It's okay, it's okay, Daph. This is just … not ideal," Margot comforted.

"No, it's not. Especially not for Leo," Astrid pointed out waving everyone out of their sleeping bags and into their morning tasks.

"A little rain's not going to take me down, Astrid," Leo rolled his eyes.

"No, maybe not, but we can't build a great fire to warm up when there's a little rain can we?" she retorted.

"I'll go look for some dry branches under the trees over there," Max offered, heading over to the forest.

Eventually the group got a big enough fire going to heat some water for the oatmeal, but it was too small to warm the soggy chill they all felt in their bones. If Margot was feeling it, she knew Leo was too and that worried her.

They got on their way quickly, preferring the tree covered path to the clearing. Daphne cracked jokes and Max told stories to keep the mood up. There was still an optimistic energy to the group, everyone agreeing that a light drizzle could easily be ignored. But Leo was shivering hard and Margot could see the worry lines on Astrid's face get deeper and deeper: as the hike progressed so did the heaviness of the rain.

By early afternoon the rain was coming down in sheets and Margot could barely see Max and Astrid trekking up the path in front of her. The final day of the hike had begun with an excitement that melted into misery as the sky became darker and the drizzle of the morning became an onslaught of rain in the afternoon. They had packed ponchos, but the raindrops managed to slip between their cracks and seep in the fabric of their pants and socks. Soggy and cold, they persevered in silence.

Margot felt the same concern she knew all the others had looming over them: Leo. He was hanging in the back of the group with Daphne holding his arm and telling him nonsense stories to keep him present. Oftentimes Margot would look back and wouldn't find them right behind her but one or two minutes down the slope. They would pause every few minutes and wait for Leo, who stumbled tentatively across every stone and root of the trail.

His eyes were ringed with purple, the same color of his lips and fingers. His red cheeks, Margot would usually attribute to Daphne's closeness, indicated his fever was still lingering. When she couldn't see him behind her, she could hear his coughing over the downpour. The rain only exasperated his illness. Margot sped up to Max and Astrid.

"If we don't reach the peak soon I think we need to pull off to the side and put a tent up for him," she mentioned quietly.

"Max and I were thinking that, too. He's looking the worst he's been and he's only getting slower and slower," Astrid agreed.

"To be honest with you, Marg, I'm not just worried about him anymore. This seems really serious. I think we need to talk about waiting out the storm," Max added, concern flickering in his eyes.

"Yes but … it's definitely not stopping anytime tonight," Margot looked up at the expanse of gray. She saw in the other two's eyes the same thought she had. Astrid finally said it out loud.

"The reality of it all is that, yes, Marg, three days may not be a possibility right now. The peak is not close by any means and it's already five in the afternoon. Visibility's awful, we're all shivering, Leo's on the verge of collapse. Daph might have to give it up." And as much as she hated the idea of the wish and the hike in the first place, Margot could see the genuine sadness in her face at the idea of missing their goal by a day.

"I'm going to go talk to them. I'll let you know," Margot smiled and turned back down the mountain. It was a while that she had to brace herself down the slope before she reached Daphne and Leo.

"Hey," Daphne smiled up at her as she emerged from the shower and mist.

"Hey," Margot's words got caught in her throat, her greeting tight with the anxiety of telling Daphne what the group had thought about.

"Heeey," Leo looked up, smiling weakly and waving a hand haphazardly in Margot's direction.

"Hi Leo, Daph. Max and Astrid and I were thinking about how you're doing and how we're all feeling and … and we think it might be best if we find some clear ground and set up camp."

"For the night?" Daphne looked offended.

"For however long it takes to wait out the storm," Margot gave a pleading grin.

"No. No, absolutely not. I'm not letting my condition keep everyone from getting their wish. We've already made it so far. We can't stop the momentum, we're almost there," Leo shouted, a frail shout that did not convince Margot of anything.

"Listen, you know I want this as much as you two. This trip has meant so much to me and I want to reach our goal. But Leo, it took me five minutes to walk back down to you two from our pace. This isn't good for you right now. You need to be warm and dry," Margot found a sternness in her voice she didn't often have and she let it show Leo how much this mattered to her.

Leo went quiet and Daphne dropped her gaze for a moment then decided it was up to him. Eventually, after some thought, Leo agreed and the group found a clearing a few minutes later to camp at.

Leo was set up in one tent, wrapped in both his and Max's sleeping bag, Daphne's blanket, and Astrid's coat which she insisted she didn't need. The rest of the group huddled in the other tent, giving Leo his space to rest. The rain persisted.

"It's not sounding great," Max gazed at the damp tent walls.

"No, it's not," Astrid rubbed her hands together, blowing on them for warmth.

"The rain really had to choose the coldest day to come down, didn't it?" Margot giggled into the tense environment in hopes of clearing the air. Daphne didn't look up, curled in her sweatshirt, knees tucked to chest, face glowering.   After some silence Astrid put her hands down and turned to her.

"Just say what you want to say, Daph. We all know you're thinking through this just like us." Daphne looked up then, mouth pinched, staring at them all.

"I know y'all don't feel super strongly about if we make it in time. Either way we had our fun, right? But I care about this. It doesn't feel right to not get there in time. And you know who else cares? Leo. He hasn't stopped talking about how excited he is to make his wish. Walking with him today, he was so scared, you don't even understand. He was so scared he was going to be a burden. He wouldn't stop asking me if everyone was mad at him and if everyone hated him for getting sick, for being the weak-link—" Daphne stopped, chin trembling and out of breath.

"Oh, Daph…" Margot breathed, scooching over to hug her, Daphne embracing her back.

"I need him to know he hasn't done anything wrong. I want him to be the first on that peak and I want it to be today. If we don't finish this, he's going to feel so insanely guilty, I just know it. He's going to blame himself," she argued, head tucked into Margot's shoulder. Margot rubbed her hair. Astrid shook her head.

"Daph … I know you feel like that's the right thing but … he's so sick ,it's not safe, it's—"

"I think we should finish it," Max broke in. "What is it like three more miles? If we all help him, it'll be over soon as we know it. He needs this, Astrid. I think we all do." He was determined, free of his apprehension and pessimism. Leo's feelings mattered more.

"Max is right. I'm in. Rain or shine I want to finish what we started," Margot nodded to Max and smiled down at Daphne. Daphne turned to Astrid.

"What do you say?" There was a long pause as Astrid thought. In the furrowing and unfurrowing of her brow, Margot could see her battle against the part of her that begged for control and rule following and smart decisions. But the side of her that put her friends and their wild ideas above all else won.

"Okay. Let's do it."

They let Leo rest for a while longer, until the sun had begun, ever so slightly, to set. Then, they woke him from his tower of blanketing and told him their plan.

"Really, you guys? You mean it?" His eyes were so excited Margot almost cried right there in the tent.

"Of course," Astrid smiled at him and handed him his poncho. The crew packed up the small camp quickly and geared up for the wet journey ahead. While Leo slept they had each transferred the heaviest items in his pack to their own making his journey a little lighter. The rain did not have that same courtesy, however, and continued to pour mercilessly down on the band of youth.

As they trekked up the final three miles of trail, they soon found attempting to converse over the rain was futile. But Margot could feel the hope in everyone through the smiles that never faded from their faces as they grappled over small boulders and slipped across muddy paths. It occurred to her that this was all intentional. The pouring rain, the difficult terrain, the lack of tree cover: the mountain was searching for the most caring part of their souls to present themselves. That part that sacrifices comfort and fear for a friend. That human commitment to one another.

All at once the path was widening and the sparse trees were growing sparser. There was the gray and rumbling sky turning Baptisia indigo with the setting of the sun. She heard Astrid laugh at the front of the path and she watched Daphne squeeze Leo's hand. She turned to Max beside her and they shared a grin.

And she started running. Max followed and then Astrid and Leo and Daphne and they sprinted to the peak. That peak they had fought for. That peak this was all for. They all paused for Leo to reach it first, his sick body running into the bright, soft light of late early night.

"I wish for this forever!" Leo shouted out, head leaned back to the sky, letting the rain shower his face.

"Me too!" Daphne grabbed his hand and shouted to the sky.

"Forever!" Margot shouted, taking Daphne's hand in hers.

"Forever!" Max screamed, hand lacing with Margot's.

"And ever," Astrid smiled, taking Max's hand and leaning her face into the on pour.

Were they tears or rain? None of them will admit to crying at that moment but none of them deny it either. And maybe the rain was their tears, falling down over this mountain for what they had had together, what they have together now and how it will change very soon and very suddenly.

"It wasn't true," Daphne said quietly, after some time of them sitting together, in their usual circle, under a tree growing atop the peak.
"Sorry?" Margot leaned closer, none of them had heard her.
"The story, it wasn't true," Daphne said, louder this time. Their faces were all stunned, staring at Daphne, her wet hair hanging around her face, bangs stuck to her forehead. "I made it up because … because I was selfish. I was scared that these last few weeks you all would be so caught up in preparing to leave and getting your things together and all that that you might forget about me, about us. This hike, it was like this world I could be with you in without distractions. I'm sorry." She looked down in her lap, embarrassed.
"Thank you for your lie, Daphne," Max smiled. "You don't know how much I needed this." A small smile formed on Daphne's face.
"You dirty liar, I love you so much," Astrid, sitting beside her, grabbed her for a hug.
"Look where your lie got me," Leo sniffled, gesturing to himself and they all laughed. "You're the best, Daph." He gave her a massive grin.
"I don't see anything to be sorry for. Yours is the kindest lie ever told," Margot squeezed her from the opposite side of Astrid.
"I cannot express how much I'm going to miss you guys. Fuck," Daphne sobbed, wiping tears from her eyes and laughing. ♛

Taylor Winstead '24

(i'm sorry)

Kiersten Hackman '24

drink,
she said.
but her hands
could not hold the cup to her lips

Margaret Jester '24

Mirabelle Smaini '26

candids in the garden, *Grayson Auman '25*

the beauty of joy, *Grayson Auman '25*

acknowledgments

Special thanks are due to the Exurbia staff who contribute their time, creativity, ideas, and passion for art throughout the year. We're also grateful for the Student Events Committee's leadership and collaboration in making this year's Art Gala happen; we're excited to have partners in celebrating the incredible art created within our community. Thanks as always to the DA OIT team for support and troubleshooting with technology; this year's journal would not exist in physical form without the help of Anne Benson. And to our amazing faculty: thanks for making space for creativity in the classroom and for encouraging our young artists to share their voice and vision. Above all, we are thankful to the writers and artists included here for choosing to create and share their original work, and to you, the reader and viewer, who have chosen to give your time and attention to art in a world so full of distraction.

Made in the USA
Columbia, SC
30 April 2024